ThePainted Lady

Books by Kee Briggs

Third Removed
The Painted War
Finders-Keepers
Losers-Weepers

The Usher Orlop Mysteries

The Golden Janus
The Pewter Masks
The Nickel Trophy
The Bronze Bones
The Brass Portraits
The Zinc Ormolu
The Silver Scepter
The Rhodium Dragon

The Asti Fantasies

Charm Catcher
Dream Weaver

Ebook

Write to Live Longer

The Painted Lady

Kee Briggs

Keescapes Publishing
Satellite Beach, Florida

The Painted Lady

Keescape Publishing books may be ordered through bookselllers or by contacting:

Keescapes Publishing
90 Flamingo Dr.
Satellite Beach, Florida 32937
www.keescapes.com
keescapespublishing@gmail.com
This is a work of fiction. All of the characters, names, incidents, organizations and dialoge are figments of the author's imagination or used fictiously.

ISBN: 978-0-9820044-2-5
Published in the United States of America

The Painted Lady

Kee Briggs

CHAPTER 1

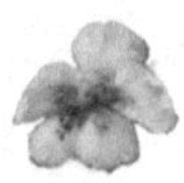

Zain was on a fishing expedition. He needed a nude model for his Monday life drawing class at Beaux Arts Academy. His regular stable of bodies had all become unavailable by taking full time jobs, moving out of the area and one had just picked up a jealous boyfriend.

So, on Thursday, he was treading the school halls checking the bulletin boards where financially strapped students advertised their willingness to shelve their modesty for the few paltry dollars the school paid for bare flesh. The only notice he found, he recognized. He did not want to have to look at that hunk of fat for three hours. The one time he'd hired her, he'd had to listen to barbed jokes from his students for weeks.

Zain pressed on to Devon's sculpture class. This wasn't Devon's figure modeling session but he might have a model name he'd be willing to share.

Devon was helping a student find the best sculptural balance on a piece of popcorn that the student had selected for his inspiration. Zain waited by the door until the instructor was able to get away.

"Hi, Zain. What brings you all the way into the city on

a Thursday? You stocking up for the big storm? Hear it's going to be a dandy."

"I plan to pick up a few things before going home, but I'm pretty well stocked up on everything I'll need. The reason I'm here today is that my model flaked out on me. I need one for Monday.

"If that storm dumps the rain on us that they are forecasting, there may not be school on Monday. We're in a low spot and if the river gets too high we'll have to be here sandbagging."

"Well, on the chance there's a class on Monday, I'll need a model. Do you have any suggestions?"

"Umm. I had a new girl all week. She's an excellent model....a pro. She can really hold a pose and she's a looker too. Cast your eyes on this." Devon walked to a storage area at the side of the room and unwrapped an eighteen inch clay figure. It was a fair representation of what appeared to be a well-proportioned, nicely muscled female.

"Hey, she looks great. Can you give me her number?"

"She doesn't have a number. She's a transient. But she hangs out during the day in the student coffee shop. She is planning on moving on, but she was worried about the storm. Try the coffee shop. She's wearing faded jeans and an orange shirt, and her pony tail is pulled through a hole in a tiny Mexican sombrero. She's an interesting model."

The last statement was said with a big grin on his face. Zain was immediately suspicious. Devon had a well-deserved reputation of being a big-time joker.

"What do you mean, 'interesting'?"

"You'll see." Devon retreated into his room full of students, still wearing that broad grin.

She must have some psychological quirk, thought Zain. The clay sculpture didn't show her with two heads or three breasts.

The model was easy to spot by her ponytail accouterment.

She was sitting alone with her elbows on the table, holding a coffee mug just below eye level. She was staring through the big window at the billowing clouds. A large back-pack was lying beside her. She had a leg through one of the shoulder straps.

"An experienced traveler," thought Zain as he sidled around the room to the serving line where he picked up a mug of coffee. That way he would approach the girl, who appeared to be in her mid-twenties, from the front instead of the rear.

As he approached, the girl's attention shifted from the clouds to him.

"Hi, I'm Zain Zook. I teach one of the life drawing classes here. Devon, the sculpture instructor, recommended you as a model. I'm looking for someone for Monday. Would you be available?"

The girl motioned for him to sit down. "Hi, I'm Rose. I've been sitting here trying to decide what to do. I'd planned on pushing west, but that would be right into the teeth of this storm and that is no fun when one is hitch-hiking."

"Hitchhiking? I didn't think people did that anymore. How can you risk hitchhiking?"

"Money."

"Money?" Zain felt like an idiot repeating what she said.

"Buses are getting terribly expensive. Besides you have to eat in those horrid, over-priced cafeterias. They don't want you to bring you're own. You have to sneak food in to eat it and I don't like to sneak."

Zain had been looking over Rose during their conversation. For some time he had been planning a series of sculptures depicting female athletes using a towel as a prop. He'd never started the series because he hadn't found the right physical form. The more he looked at Rose, the more excited he was becoming. He may have found the perfect physique for his project.

Since money was an important consideration at the

moment, Zain tossed out another inducement. I'm a sculptor. I've been planning a series of pieces and I think you might be the proper model for the series. If you'll stay over for the Monday class, I'll pay you for a couple of private sessions this weekend."

"Those private sessions....are you thinking about having them here or in your studio? You do have a studio don't you?"

"Oh, yes, a very good one, even if I say so myself. I hadn't thought about that yet. Before I go further, I need to know if you'd permit photos.

"Let me explain. My thesis concerned the use of photos to capture action in figurative sculpture. I have a formula for getting all the angles so when I sculpt I have a complete visual reference.

"For a long time there was no problem dealing with nude photographs. Now, every time someone sees a 'necked' lady, he or she reports it and the sculptor is declared to be a pervert. I began processing my own film to keep out of trouble. Now the digital camera has simplified everything. I can print from the computer. Nothing leaves my control."

"How much do you pay?"

"Twice the regular school modeling fee."

"I'll make you an offer. You pay me one hundred bucks, feed me and provide me with a bed and I'll model all weekend. Then I'll model on Monday for the school fee.

"Before you agree to this, let me tell you that this is not a weekend stand. I'll not go to bed with you nor tolerate any unprofessional conduct. Can you accommodate a weekend house guest or will your wife give you grief?"

"No wife and yes, I can handle a weekend guest. I have a big place. There's no problem there. Also, I have a reputation to maintain at the school. I'll not pull anything funny."

"I'm only making such an offer because I don't want to sleep in the park or under a bridge with a big storm coming."

"Well, if you're ready, we'd better leave. I have some shopping to do and with another mouth to feed, I'd better lay in some more food. Are you a meat eater or a veggie lover?"

"I like veggies and fruit, but I eat meat when I can afford it."

Zain opened the side door of his van so Rose could put her pack out of the way.

"This is a tank," said Rose, as she took the big step up.

"My place is out of town and there are some hills. Besides, I'm always carrying sculpture supplies. I have my own foundry, which takes a lot of feeding."

The next destination was the grocery store. Rose followed him down the aisles. Zain picked up a supply of eggs, bacon and sausage. His pass by the meat counter netted some steaks, a pork loin cut into chops, and a ham. He also threw a large bag of dry cat food and another of dog food under the cart.

Zain let Rose pick the vegetables and fruits. He noted that she chose the ones in local season, avoiding the pricey imports.

A large pack of batteries and a couple of new flashlights were added. "There is only one power line down the valley and it goes out occasionally. One needs to be prepared.

The bill was sizeable when they got to the check stand. Rose looked apprehensive until Zain paid in cash without comment.

Even though it was mid-afternoon, the light was poor. Zain left town on a county highway. Eight miles later, he turned off on a gravel road that ran up a broad valley with a small river meandering its way down the valley.

Zain asked his passenger how she had gotten into modeling.

"Oh, I've been around art all my life. My dad was a

commercial artist. My mother was a china painter.

"When I went to college, I roomed with an art student and occasionally modeled for him. After we split up, I worked at the art school for extra spending money." There was a long pause. "Then mom died and my schooling came to a halt."

"Why?"

"Money."

"Money?" There, he did it again.....Idiot.

"I didn't know what a sacrifice Mom was making to send me to school. Dad had improved his status many years earlier by moving in with the owner of his biggest account. As soon as he could, he married her.

"I thought dad had provided for my education, but Mom was working two jobs and selling all her nice things to keep me fat, dumb and happy. When Mom died there wasn't anything left. I don't even have a piece of her hand painted china. She sold everything."

Rose slumped down in her seat and was silent.

Zain continued driving down the gravel road. After a considerable time, he pointed out, "There's my only neighbor." Sitting on the edge of the flat river plain with the hills rising behind was a cluster of buildings. The scene was dominated by a big, red barn in the background and a large, rambling farmhouse in the foreground. Part of the house was two-storied, and there appeared to have been many additions.

The place was a scene of intense activity. There were animals of all sorts running about. Rose spotted regular chickens, funny-looking chickens, white geese, Muscovies, several guinea hens, and even peahens. There were several four-footed critters, such as goats, pigs, and a llama. Then there were the kids. They all seemed intent on chores....not play.

Zain passed along with a toot of the horn. "That's my place."

Sitting on a bench overlooking the river was an enormous, two storied house with two front garrets. A long lane led up the hill to the front porch. The lane was lined with dead and dying poplars. The formal entry was a scraggly mess.

Rose had instant misgivings about her weekend arrangement. Backed by the bleak, foreboding sky and with the weathered exterior, the house looked like something out of a horror movie.

Zain saw his passenger recoil upon seeing the house.

"Don't let the appearance scare you. I inherited the place from a couple of old-maid aunts. It was their family estate since before the turn of the century. Oh, there have been several upgrades since it was built. There is interior plumbing and central heating. There are even modern appliances in the kitchen."

"You live here alone?"

"Yep. Just me and Wolf, the dog and, Nutsy, the tomcat. At one time there were a large number of pedigreed horses and a stable to accommodate them. That's where I've set up my studio. My foundry is behind."

Zain drove up the long rutted driveway between the ratty poplars. He bypassed the grand front entry to go around the house. "We'll park by the kitchen to unload all this food. We'd better hurry, it's starting to rain."

Zain pulled up to a small, elevated back porch. As he got out of the van, he pulled an old- fashioned latch-key from his pocket. He unlocked the door and propped it open with an antique flat iron. "Welcome to the lair."

Rose was still apprehensive about her bargain. She was a long way from anywhere. The place still looked like a haunted house. In the service porch wires ran along the ceiling and the walls from little bakelite switches to porcelain light fixtures.

The kitchen more modern. It was the biggest kitchen she'd ever seen outside of a hotel. It looked like two single-car garages hooked end-to-end. Half of it housed two wood stoves with stove-pipes going into brick chimneys. There were several freestanding side-boards with tin bins beneath. The other half of the kitchen was from the modern world. There were white appliances—an electric range and oven, refrigerator, upright freezer, microwave oven and assorted other small appliances and Formica cabinet tops. The sight of familiar appliances reduced the heart palpitations somewhat.

Zain supervised the stashing of groceries in their proper places. "Before it gets any darker and it rains any harder, let me show you my studio." Zain could see his model was ill at ease, probably wondering if she'd been conned into something for which she would be sorry.

He led the way through a cluster of smaller buildings. He pointed to one behind the kitchen. "That was the carriage house. It's too small for any standard car. Maybe you could squeeze a Miata in."

There were old chicken hutches and rabbit pens scattered about. They approached a big building, which Zain referred to as the stables. There were two large sliding doors in the middle under a haymow at the peak. To the left was a passage door with a modern lock. Zain unlocked the door and stepped inside to flip a light switch.

"This is the old tack room. It was beautifully finished. I just had to move out all the horsey things to make my clean-room. Any dirty work goes on in one of the stables.

The foundry is in a block building I built behind. You can't have molten bronze in a building like this."

"You really do have a studio," said Rose without taking council of her words.

"You thought I was spoofing you?"

"Oh, no, I just didn't think it would be anything like this." Rose was irritated with herself for such an inane comment and such a lame reply.

In the middle of the room was a 5'x5' platform, a foot high, covered with brown carpet. A number of flood lights were focused on the stand. Zain caught Rose eyeing the setup. "That'll be your throne for the next couple of days."

Zain's comment was interrupted by a nearby clap of thunder. That was followed by the sound of huge raindrops pelting down on the outer walls..

"Run for it," cried Zain. Rose headed for the house while Zain delayed just long enough to turn out the lights and shut the door.

By the time they got to the house, they both were soaked. They pounded up the steps and into the mud room where they laughingly stripped water off their arms and hair.

Zain led the way into the kitchen. The laughter continued when they spotted a perfectly dry cat and dog sitting in the middle of the room studying the two drenched arrivals.

"At least you don't raise any dumb animals around here," said Rose.

Zain patted the dog on the head. "This is Wolf. He is not named for his pedigree, but his eating habits. His lineage is indeterminate. He was a stray that showed up one day.... half starved. His eating hasn't slowed down yet.

"And who is this handsome guy?" asked Rose.

"That's Nutsy." One day I was sitting at the kitchen table sketching and he walked in the door, minutely inspected the kitchen and all the rooms that were open. The place must have met his specifications because he hopped up on the window sill and went to sleep in the sun. He usually walks with his tail straight up in the air. You'll notice the source of his name when he walks away from you."

Rose rolled her eyes up to look at Zain. Then she turned the cat, which had been sideswiping her leg, around so she could see the two chocolate brown balls on an otherwise totally white cat.

Zain quelled an impulse to pick up Rose's backpack.

Instead, he said, “Grab you pack and I’ll show you to your room so you can change out of those wet things.

By then, it was pitch black outside. The rain was slicing nearly horizontally, slamming the windows on the windward side. The wind was moaning through the decorative devices under the eaves.

Zain led the way through the family dining room. Sliding open the doors into the central hall, Zain snapped on the lights.

“Wow,” exclaimed Rose at the width and length of the central hallway.

“As you come in the front door,” said Zain, “the room to the right is the formal parlor where guests are entertained. To the left is the less formal family parlor. The second door on the right is the music room. Across the hall is the library. Next to it is the formal dining room. We just passed through the family breakfast, lunch and dinner facility. When extra ranch help was needed, the hands ate in the kitchen.”

“How many people used to live here?”

“Old man Graff had high hopes. When he built it, he expected his kids would bring their families to live here....if not in the big house, somewhere on the ranch. This would be the grand meeting hall. The eldest was a boy. Alonso was the foundation of Graff’s immortality, but he got killed in a freak accident when he was twenty-five years old.”

“There were only three in this monstrous place?”

“No. There were also two sisters.. Oh, there were also numerous servants at one time.”

“It boggles my mind to think of so few with so much.”

Zain assiduously shied away from politics, and that last comment had all the fervor of a raging liberal. To avoid getting involved in the philosophical rights and wrongs of wealth, Zain headed up the stairs. “The bedrooms are all up here.”

The six-foot-wide staircase rose from the center of the

grand hallway, leaving four feet on either side for access to the rear portion of the house.

On the second floor, Zain veered left. "This was one sister's bedroom. I use the other one across the hall." A musty smell oozed out as the door opened.

Rose was pleasantly surprised to find a much more up-to-date room than the house indicated.

"Each sister decorated in her own taste. This was the pink lady. The other one favored green. I chose the green one. I keep this one up as a guest room, but as you can tell from the smell, I don't have many house guests."

Rose eyed the huge, old-fashioned four-poster bed with a pink canopy. When she dropped her backpack on the bed, it sagged nicely. She'd feared it would be one of those old, hard things she'd read about.

Zain laughed. "The bed looks old, but the springs and mattress are premium quality king-sized jobs. I'd like to air the room out, but this is the windward side of the house. I'm afraid we'd be awash if I cracked the window."

"I'll leave the door open. That should help."

"Come along. I'll show you the bathroom. There is only one in the house. We'll have to make some arrangements."

At the end of the hall was a new wall with a door in the middle. Zain stepped through the open door and turned on the lights.

Rose giggled. "What is this?"

"The sister were twins. They apparently weren't concerned about mutual modesty, but they had a thing about commingling toiletries. Two rooms, plus the hallway were converted into a duel bathroom."

Straight ahead were two washer-and-drier sets. The rest of the end wall was full of closets and built-in drawers. On each sidewall was a large glass-enclosed shower, double-sink vanities with mirrors, a toilet and a bidet.

"Each had her own towels, wash clothes, sheets, and so

forth. Each had her own washer so as not to let the pink bleed into the green. They could each sit on the pot and talk to one another, but never should their bath towels meet. There was even pink and green toilet paper when I first came."

Rose shook her head. "Strange ladies."

"There's a door from each bedroom plus the hall door. I suppose we should knock before entering. Sound off if you're in here, so I don't walk in on you at a bad time."

"I'm not prudish enough for that to bother me, but I'll do as you say. I get the pink side?"

"Right. Pink's not my color."

"Okay, clear out. I need to try out the facilities."

"I'm going to change clothes and head for the kitchen to feed the menagerie."

CHAPTER 2

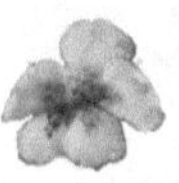

Zain was fussing around the kitchen when Rose reappeared. She'd changed jeans and top. Her hair was rolled in a pink towel, which was one of the ideas for his lady and towel series.

"The tentative menu is spicy pork chops, pan gravy over boiled potatoes and veggies of your choice."

"Sounds great to me. I'll take care of the veggies."

While Zain was putting the potatoes on to boil, he said, "Where are you going from here?"

"I'm headed for Seattle. I'm not on a particularly tight schedule, but I have to get there. I usually move as the money permits."

"Is Seattle a destination or just another stop?"

"Don't know yet. I'm going to Seattle to have my tattoo-guy put on the final panel. If I find anything worth staying for, I'll stay. If not, I'll look elsewhere."

"You've got tattoos?"

"Yep, wait till you see them."

"Devon said you were interesting. Was that what he was

referring to?"

"I have no idea. Maybe he was referring to my personality," said Rose with a laugh. "Will tattoos bother your artistic endeavors?"

"No, not mine. They might distract a painter, but I'm not as concerned about surface as the two dimensional people."

"You said you were planning a series. What kind of series?"

"Ever since the last summer Olympics, I've been thinking about investigating people and how they use a towel. There was a female sprinter who didn't medal. She stood with her head down. She had a towel behind her neck. She had both ends in her hands and she was pulling down. The towel added to her abjection.

"Yet another girl won. She had the towel hooked behind her head and her hand lifted the ends of the towel toward the sky. The towel was part of her victory. The towel tied around your head is another icon of modern life."

Zain got his part of the dinner cooking. He turned the drain board over to Rose. "Your turn."

Zain sat back at the the small table in the modern half of the kitchen. When the coffee pot stopped grumbling, Zain poured two cups. He deposited one on the counter top and retreated with the other to the table, where he continued to inspect his new model. He already know her vital statistics....5'7", slender, long, tapered muscles, B cup, short waist, long legs, medium shoe size, long, light brown hair, straight. Now he was watching her movements, looking for natural positions, graceful movements, and markedly individual habits.

He liked what he saw, although the thoughts of tattoos bothered him. Tattooing was probably the last thing that he'd ever permit being done to his body. He found satisfaction when he heard the Japanese looked upon tattooing as the mark of a criminal. The positive points of his model far outweighed any tattooing. He'd be gentlemanly and refrain from making any of his normal comments concerning people who subject themselves to such idiocies.

Rose steamed broccoli in the microwave and topped it with raw shoestring carrots she had made on Zain's plastic mandolin.

After dinner and an exchange of compliments, they did the dishes and then adjourned to the family parlor where there was a large TV set. They watched the news reports concerning the monster storm, which was roaring down on them from the Pacific Northwest. There were flood warnings being issued for all low-lying locations and flash flood warnings for the high country. The size and the severity of the storm were predicted to reach high enough to meet some of the high mountain perpetual snow pack and cause a melt-off.

When the image started to break up and the dish announced it was seeking the satellite, Zain said, "The storm sounds like it is getting worse. The electricity will probably go out next. We'd better get ready for a blackout. It won't be so bad. This house was built before there was any electricity in this area."

Zain led the way into the kitchen. He was just handing Rose one of the newly purchased flashlights when the lights went out. A gasp came from Rose.

"Follow me," said Zain as he switched on his flashlight. He led the way through a door at the end of the old kitchen. There was a long hallway with numerous closed door. The end room was lined with shelves holding dozens of oil lamps.

"This room is vented to carry away part of the stink. I never did like the smell of coal oil."

"Is that another name for kerosene?"

"Yeah. It still stinks by any other name. But it keeps us

out of the dark. Here, take these two lamps. A house policy is that a lamp has to be filled before it is put back on the shelf."

The pair retreated to the kitchen. Zain used a butane fireplace starter to light one of the lamps. He adjusted the wick to stop the smoking.

"You've got to tend these to keep from smoking up the house. When you go up to bed, take this up with you. There's a bracket beside the door. Be sure to put it out before going to sleep. Oh, here are some matches in case you need to relight it. Probably, the flashlight will be all you need."

"How long do these summer storms usually last?" said Rose, who was feeling quite apprehensive about her entire situation.

"Usually, they blow over in a day or two, but the weather people say this is much more intense than normal. Don't worry, we're high and dry. How about a beer while they are still cold? I don't like warm suds."

"That sounds good to me."

Zain pulled a couple of cans from the refrigerator. "There are plenty more in there. I can only handle a couple before I feel bloated. But, help yourself to as many as you want."

Wolf snuggled down against Zain's shoe. Much to Zain's surprise, Nutsy came out from his hidey-hole and jumped into Rose's lap.

"You see," said Rose, "cats can recognize a cat lover when they meet one. He's even got his motor going."

Two beers later, both decided it was time to retire. Zain coached his guest on lamp care and feeding again before disappearing into his own room.

CHAPTER 3

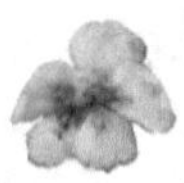

Dawn seemed late in coming because of the black clouds and driving rain. Zain bumped and banged around the bathroom enough to make his presence known and then headed downstairs. Rose followed along shortly.

She found Zain sitting at a small table in the old end of the kitchen. A fire was crackling in one of the two large, wood cook stoves. A blue, enameled coffee pot was working toward boiled coffee.

"Good morning," said Rose brightly.

"You're quite chipper for such a dark and dismal day."

"I survived the night. No ghosts showed up. I didn't hear any clanking chains. The storm didn't blow the roof off and sleeping in the big pink bed is like sleeping on a cloud. All my fears are behind me....let's have fun." She didn't mention that she hadn't had to fight off her host in the middle of the night.

Wolf became alert. Nutsy jumped down from Rose's lap just before a resounding knock from the front of the house reverberated down the hallway.

Through the etched glass of the front door Zain recognized

the silhouette of his neighbor, Bo Vasa.

Bo didn't waste any time with small talk. "Sorry to bother you so early, but I came to ask permission to cut your wire and to get my livestock onto your high ground. The river's rising fast. I brought the cattle and horses across the ford last night, but the pasture on this side will be under water before too long."

Bo was talking fast. Rose came to stand beside Zain. "Ma'am." After acknowledging Rose's presence he turned back to Zain. "I have a little transistor radio. The morning report says the highest dam up river is showing signs of weakness. If it goes, the two lower ones may go too, flooding the entire valley. I've got to get my livestock to safety."

"No problem," said Zain. "Cut the wire. I haven't been around long enough to know, but if the valley floods, won't that get your house too?"

"As soon as I can get the livestock safe, we're going to move as much as possible to the upper floor. I don't think the water can reach the second floor."

"Need any help with the livestock?"

"No. The wife and kids and I can manage. How big an area is that?"

"There's about 350 acres in the piece, but it's fenced in. The critters can wander, but they can't get out."

"Got to go. Thanks."

"Yell if you need some help."

Rose and Zain went back to their coffee.

"Those poor people," said Rose. "They stand to lose a whole lot. They may keep their livestock, but to lose their home and all their belongings.... I'd hate to lose my backpack. I travel light, but that stuff means a lot to me."

"How are you at making bacon and eggs? If you can get them going, I'll go out to see if I can get the old tractor going in case we need it."

"I can handle that. How many eggs?"

"Two....over easy. Give me ten minutes."

In the mud-room, Zain picked a yellow raincoat off the peg. He clapped on a broad- brimmed cowboy hat, which he nearly lost as soon as he stepped out into the wind. He retreated into the mud room to change into black, rubber boots.

Against the wind driven rain, Zain made it to one of the outbuildings. Fortunately, the big double-doors were on the lee of the building. Parked in the middle of the shed was a majestic, old Titan tractor with two large, steel wheels with steel cleats. Zain had periodically fired up the behemoth just to keep it in running condition. He flipped the on switch and check to make sure it was in neutral before putting his back into turning the fly wheel. It fired on the second try. The phrase, "They don't make them like they used to" passed through his head as he listened to the roar. With an adjustment to the magneto the engine settled down to a regular beat.

Zain turned off the tractor and sloshed back to the house. He could smell the bacon from the mud room as he dumped his rain gear. As he entered the kitchen, Rose poured four eggs from a bowl into a skillet.

"Sounded as if you were successful. What is that loud thing?"

"It's an ancient farm tractor, but perfectly maintained. It'll go anywhere except on a side hill. There is a big, four-wheeled hay trailer in the shed behind the barn. There's no sense in the Vasas hoping the water won't get to them on the second floor. I'm going to offer them the choice of staying here. We can load their stuff on the trailer and store it in the barn. The water'll never get up there."

"How many are in the family?"

"I'm not sure. There's six or eight kids. Some may have to sleep on the floor, but that's better than being in harm's way."

"What about food? That's a lot of people."

"They've probably stocked up. We'll bring it along. They can cook it here. There's no problem with the water. I have a spring-fed cistern up the hill. It's gravity fed. You can even take a hot shower. The water tank is a propane job."

"This should be some experience. How are you with kids?"

"Never been around many before. I was an only child."

"Me too."

"Oh, we'll survive a couple/three days."

Rose slid the eggs onto a couple of plates, and added the bacon and fried toast.

"You do that well," said Zain.

Rose laughed. "I do a lot of things. I've cooked over campfires for years. And my checkered work history includes short-order cook. Eat before it gets cold and greasy."

Zain refilled the coffee cups before the pair did away with breakfast.

"With no electricity, there's a lot in the fridge that needs eating before it spoils," said Zain. "Let's use as much as possible. I'm going to take the tractor down to the Vasa house."

"I'm going, too. They'll need all the help they can get. Do you have another rain coat?"

"Yeah, there's all sorts of things in the closet off the mud room. Help yourself."

Rose found everything she needed in abundance. She settled on a pink raincoat, southwester and rubber boots. She did a fashion twirl as she came back into the kitchen.

Zain laughed. "The pink twin must have been your size. Let's go."

After Zain backed the behemoth out of the shed, Rose closed the doors and climbed up beside the driver. She kept a leery eye on the wicked-looking steel wheel rotating inches away.

They hooked the hay wagon behind the tractor before they crawled down the hill. Zain was careful not to churn up his road. It was already muddy enough. The wind-pushed rain made little wet spots all over their bodies. They were both shivering by the time they turned into the Vasa driveway.

Their arrival was no surprise because the tractor challenged the storm noise as soon as it was started. The whole family was up the hill driving the last of the cattle through the fence onto Zain's property. Bo was using wire and a 2x4 to fashion the barbed wire into a gate. The rest of the family charged down the hill to greet the visitors. They arrived in age order. The youngest ones first. The older kids descended the hill at a more dignified gait. The two youngest ones gamboled along with the tractor like a couple of fillies.

Mrs. Vasa veered off toward the back door, waving for the new arrivals to come in. Everyone shed dripping rain gear before going into the large country kitchen. Zain introduced the two women, and Carina named the eight kids that gathered about.

Carina poured coffee from a large pot that had been kept warm on a gas stove. Some of the kids took coffee too.

"Thanks," said Zain. "We came down to invite you guys to come up and stay with us until the storm passes. There's no sense in chancing it here if those dams go. Why not pack up whatever is valuable, your clothes and food and come up? There's plenty of room. That old house is set up to handle this type of situation."

Carina looked greatly relieved, but she deferred to her husband. "That's a wonderful offer. I'll have to ask Bo. Erik, run up and help your father so he can come down. Emil, you too."

Both the older kids headed out to get their rain gear.

"Do you have water?" asked Carina.

"Plenty. It's a gravity feed spring system. I've got lots of gas for hot showers or doing dishes. We can put anything you want to store in the stable or the barn. It might get wet going up but it will stay dry once it arrives."

They fell silent as the little transistor radios began a storm report. The news was not good. Carina was definitely concerned. Driving out was already out of the question. Even before her husband arrived, she began issuing orders to the kids. The little ones were given big plastic bags for their toys.. The others started packing food stuffs. By the time Bo arrived, a full-fledged evacuation was underway.

After a brief consultation on the back porch, the Vasas reached unanimity. They would accept the invitation. Bo was being a little stiff-backed about accepting gratuitous offerings, but Zain countered that he was just being neighborly. Neighbors did for neighbors and that wasn't charity.

Zain and Rose joined the work-force. They helped Carina and Bo move furniture and household goods to the second floor. Clothing and personal items went downstairs to be bagged and stacked by the back door.

Work went at a furious pace. Bo and the oldest boys challenged the storm to get valuable equipment out of the outbuildings onto the trailer. The family van and various farm vehicles were driven through the gate to high ground. Bo's old farm truck remained next to the barn.

"What about the truck?" said Zain.

"Blew the engine last week."

"I can tow it to high ground."

"No need. It's not worth fixin'. I'm going to junk it out. It won't matter if it gets wet."

They worked straight through lunch with occasional finger snacks offered by Carina.

It was one of the kids who sound the alarm. "Look, there's no road."

Everyone rushed to the front of the house. The river

had been over its banks since dawn, but it was now rising much faster than anyone had anticipated. It was coming into the front yard.

Zain stepped out where he could see the lay of the land between the two driveways. Another possible problem became evident. Several of the old, dead poplars were no longer standing. The upwind ones were across the driveway.

"That land is too steep to traverse. We'll have to go straight up through your new gate to level ground and then across. Load the trailer."

Zain pulled the tractor to within inches of the elevated porch. He left the tractor idling.

The whole contingent fell to loading the trailer. Fifteen minutes later, Carina closed the back door and stepped onto the trailer. Zain was sure the moisture running down her face was not all rainwater. Without saying anything, Bo stepped back onto the porch and blocked the door open with a concrete block before slogging ahead to open the new wire gate. Slowly, Zain moved through the farmyard toward the high ground behind the barn. Progress came to a halt after a shriek from Inga and Inger.

In unison, the twins slid off the trailer and charged the ramp leading into the barn. They went slithering through the muck and mud to get under the ramp. Moments later, they came crawling out dragging a squealing potbelly pig. Bo helped the kids get the struggling pet aboard the trailer before the evacuation resumed.

Zain went straight uphill. The old tractor steadily clicked over, even on the most precipitous slope. When he got to the level bench on which his house sat, he made a sweeping left turn into the wind, heading for his back porch.

The unloading of the household goods went swiftly. A premature dusk settled in, adding impetus to get finished while there was still light. Zain lighted lanterns and directed that the mountain of bags go into the modern part of the kitchen, which was useless without electricity. When the unloading of household items was finished, Zain moved the tractor and trailer into the central corridor of the stables. The howling wind was a pleasant change from the infernal tractor noise.

When he got back to the house, there was a mound of rain gear in the mud room. Zain made his contribution to the mess.

In the kitchen, Carina had taken over directing where the food and allied articles should be stacked. Bo was directing the kids in sorting out bags containing items of immediate need and those that could wait until later. Rose was getting the coffee pot ready and mixing a once frozen container of orange juice concentrate for the kids.

Zain went down the back hall to the wood room where he pulled out an old battered wood box on casters. He filled it with stove wood and tossed a couple of pitch chips on top. He pushed the box into the kitchen to its age-old position between the two cook stoves. He'd been using the bigger stove as a trash-burner for any combustible debris. It was stuffed with paper. With the addition of wood and a pitch chip, there was a roaring fire in a few moments. Soon the coffee pot was heating.

Carina turned her attention to getting something to eat for the starving throng. Rose was showing signs of wearing down. She'd been soaked most of the day. Despite the relative warmth of the house she began to shiver badly.

Zain sidled up to her. "Go upstairs and get a hot shower and some dry clothes before the thundering herd gets there."

Rose gave him an appreciative nod and disappeared into the hall.

To the rest of the group he said, "When you get things sorted out, I'll show you what I can offer in sleeping accommodations. Some of the kids will probably have to sleep on the floor."

"No problem," said Bo. "They'll think they're camping."

Carina had some questions about cooking pots. The cupboard had only small containers, better fitted to a single male's cooking habits. Zain led her down to one of the back pantries, which had huge pots stacked inside even bigger pots. They were left over from when the ranch had to feed roundup crews. Carina was collecting an assortment of pots and implements when a loud keening cry ricochetted through the house passageways. Zain jumped and headed back toward the kitchen.

Carina yelled at his back. "That's one of the kids. They use that signal to call the other to see something interesting. I wonder what they're into."

It sounded like a herd of buffalo as multiple feet thundered up the stairs to the second floor.

Carina dropped her load of kettles on the drain board. Bo came in from the mud room where he had been trying to create some semblance of order with the rain gear.

"What's going on?" said Carina.

Bo shrugged.

"You shouldn't let them run around Zain's house like a bunch of mad Vikings."

Carina headed for the stairs with the two males in tow. The buzz of voices came from the bathroom. Carina went charging in. The men stopped at the door.

"What are you heathens doing?" demanded Carina. All the kids were grouped around Rose, who was standing naked in the middle of the room holding a stretched towel over her head. The kids formed a circle around her as she slowly rotated.

The only response was, "Hey, Mom, take a look at this. This is really something," said one of the boys.

Bo decided to let his wife handle the situation. Zain held

back, not wanting to get involved in a family affair. His guess was that the kids had found the mysterious tattoos. The human sea parted to let mom in. Zain got a glimpse of a continuous band of tattoos stretching around the body, a couple/three inches below the navel. As Rose rotated he could see a blank patch on the right flank."

"Have you no sense of propriety? What are you doing bothering this poor girl when she's bathing. Now get out of here."

"Aw, Mom. She doesn't care." said Inger.

"I said 'Scat'," said Carina in an ominous voice.

There was a general stampede for the door.

Rose brought the towel down and wrapped it around her chest, which also covered the tattoo.

"I'm sorry dear," said Carina. "I'm afraid we haven't quite raised those kids for polite society. You see, our bathroom is more like a school locker room with multiple facilities, that everyone can use at once. I see I'm going to have to have a few lessons on respecting the privacy of others."

"Oh, don't be too hard on them," objected Rose. "I rather like to show off my art to an appreciative audience."

"I still see that they need some instruction in propriety." Carina herded Bo and Zain out of the bathroom and closed the door. Everyone returned to his assigned chores until Carina called them to dinner.

It was a hastily put together meal of macaroni and cheese, sliced kielbasa and frozen peas, but it was well received by a ravenous throng. There was little conversation at the table because they were listening to the weather report over a transistor radio.

As the meal wound down, Zain said, "I have two bedrooms upstairs at the front of the house. Also there are a couple of davenports in the downstairs parlors. Beyond that I have plenty of floor space."

Rose broke in. "Why don't I move in with you, Zain? Then

Bo and Carina can have my room.

Zain gave her a quizzical look.

"No. This does not imply any change in our agreement."

The two older sets of twins snickered, picking up the unsaid implications. The adults politely ignored everything. The younger ones paid no attention.

Carina objected. "We can make out perfectly well without displacing you."

Zain fell in line. "I'd feel guilty occupying a king-sized bed alone."

Conversation was interrupted by thunder marching down the valley. Lightening strikes made scary patterns against the walls. One gigantic clap shook the house. Elen and Elsa shrieked as they ran to Carina. Kas and Ken moved with a little more restraint into the arms of their father. The older twins held their ground as befitting their advanced ages.

"This thunderstorm will pass in a few minutes," said Zain. "Let's get the dishes into the sink. We'll deal with them when it gets light. Now it's time to figure out sleeping arrangements." All did their bit to clear the table.

"Everyone grab his personal gear and follow me." Zain picked up the two lamps from the table and waited by the door until everyone was headed upstairs. Rose retrieved her backpack and wet towel before turning the pink bedroom over to the Vasa adults.

"Oh, there's plenty of room here. We'll put the four young ones along the wall. If this storm continues, they'll be in bed with us anyway."

Zain showed the older twins to the other bedrooms and gave them a lamp with the admonition of not going to sleep with the lamp still lit. They had a flashlight for emergency trips to the bathroom.

When Zain made it to his room, he found Rose seated in his computer chair surveying his world, which had been substantially altered from its green days. No feminine accouterments remained. It was strictly a male's domain. Browns and earthy yellows mingled with the residual green. The king-sized bed, without the decorative froufrou had been pushed into a corner next to one of the windows to make room for an extensive computer setup in the other corner. There was also a massive recliner and side table sitting in front of floor-to-ceiling bookshelves along an inner wall. It was a rather impressive display since the ceilings were twelve feet high.

Zain hustled about picking up assorted dirty clothes, shoes, and used towels and shifted them into a wardrobe. "Sorry about that." He was grateful for the dim lamp light, which he hoped covered his reddening neck.

"No problem. I like your room. I prefer pink only in certain places. I didn't mean to put you in a difficult position, but I would have not felt good about hogging that big bed when it could be put to better use."

"It makes sense to double up under the circumstances. I hadn't gotten that far beyond the moment. I hope I don't snore."

"If you do, I'll let you know."

"If you'll strip the bed, I'll get fresh sheets and another pillow." Without waiting for a reply he headed into the bathroom only to encounter a horde of naked kids washing up and brushing teeth. No one paid any attention to him as he got clean bedding out of a cupboard.

Before putting on the clean sheets, Zain pulled the bed away from the wall a couple of feet for the end table that was supposed to be there. His computer printer ended up on the floor as the table was returned to its rightful bedside position.

As the pair worked to prepare the bedroom, little was said. Zain was trying to figure out how he wanted to handle the new sleeping arrangements. One of his steadfast rules was not to display any intimacy toward any of his models, especially when they were nude. Proper self-restraint was a sign of professionalism in his book. Being as young as he was, he had to be particularly careful not to be as horny as everyone seemed to expect him to be. Oh, there were occasions when he had bedded a model, but it was always the result of proper adult interaction well after the modeling session. There had even been times when girls had modelled for him with every intent of having sex with him. They were showing off their wares. After all, he was considered to be a good catch. On these occasions, he'd always fallen back on his professional ethics to avoid even the look of impropriety.

While Zain was shuffling his clothes in the wardrobe making room for his roommate's hanging clothes, Rose began to undress. She'd pulled a straight-back chair to the wall side of the bed. Without actually watching, Zain kept track of her progress as he fussed about the room. Rose removed her boots and socks, which went under the chair. Next came the jeans, followed by the shirt. She wasn't wearing a bra....not that she needed one. That left her in a pair of high-waisted panties that covered the upper portion of the tattoo. The lower end of the tattoo extended a couple of inches below the cotton.

Rose crawled under the covers and leaned back against the headboard. She smoothed the bedding across her lap and turned her attention to Zain. "It sounds as if that storm is getting even worse."

"They say its a huge storm. It may be with us for a while."

"How high will the water get?"

"I don't know. I've never seen anything like this in the three years I've been here. Don't worry. Most of the world would have to flood before it got this high."

"I was thinking about the Vasa house."

"If it only rains, it should be all right. If the dams go that could be bad."

Zain started to undress by the recliner, which he used as a clothes rack. When he got down to his navy blue, low-rise briefs, he blew out the lamp and used the flashlight to find the bed.

He handed Rose the flashlight. "I can find my way around without it. Goodnight."

"Goodnight."

CHAPTER 4

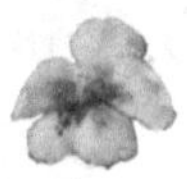

It was a peculiar night. Zain was aware of the storm and the female on the other edge of the bed and yet he thought he had slept.

Sleep was violently jerked away from him by the high, piercing keening cry, which truly was keening. When his eyes snapped open and he could see the faint, first-light edging in around the window shade, he knew what had happened. One of the kids had seen the Vasa house.

There was a general scramble toward the front bedroom. Inga and Inger were holding each other as they stared out the high, narrow window.

Everyone strained to see the angry, swirling water lap over the decking of the front porch. The house, on pillars and posts, stood higher than the sheds and barn, which already had water inside. Fortunately, there wasn't enough light to see details. A sob escaped from somewhere. The twins sought each other and Bo held his wife closely.

Carina finally straightened, pulled away from her husband and said, "Okay, kids, we knew this might happen. The important thing is that we are all high and dry. It'll take some work to put the farm back together again, but we can do it. Go get some clothes on and come down to the kitchen. We have chores to do."

Zain and Rose were overdressed for the occasion. They returned to their room. Zain rolled up the window shades to get enough light to dress.

As he pulled on his pants, he said, "Unfortunately, it will probably get worse."

Although he had been keeping his eyes averted, he knew Rose was sitting on the chair next to the bed. When he didn't get a response, he focused his eyes on his roommate. She was crying.

"Hey, you hardly know those folks."

"Does that make the loss any less?" whispered Rose.

"No. I guess not."

"I'm so glad you brought them up here. That was a really nice thing to do."

Zain was suddenly uncomfortable with that kind of praise. "Just being neighborly." It came out a little gruffer than he'd intended as he tried to cover his discomfort.

"It's still nice."

Even with the carpeted treads, the thundering herd of kids could be heard above the wrath of the storm as they headed for the kitchen.

"I'd better get down there to start the fire." Zain grabbed his boots and was out the door, leaving Rose to get dressed.

Carina already had the fire crackling. She'd banked the fire before going to bed. There was also some old, warm coffee snarling from the pot at anyone who walked by.

Breakfast was rather lavish in that Carina was cooking those items that would spoil without a refrigerator. Bo was assigning chores to the kids. The two older boys got the outside duties. Inga and Inger were to help Carina in the kitchen and with housekeeping. Kas and Ken were to keep the wood box filled and the lamps cleaned and filled. The two five-year olds were gofers.

As the light became brighter, Bo and Zain stepped out on the front porch to survey the situation in the valley. The Vasa farm was awash. There was water in the lower floor of the house. Bo had turned the chickens loose, hoping they would find shelter in the upper reaches of the barn. The rabbits would have to be evacuate. All the other animals that couldn't get through the fence had been driven through the gate.

Zain was concerned over the road and power lines. The Graff sisters brought electricity to the house at their own considerable expense. It was three miles to the public lines. To re-electrify the place will be terribly costly. Of course, the Vasas should help, but from what he could see there wasn't any excess money in that household.

Another concern was the road. It was under water. From what Zain could see, there were probable washouts. It was also a private road....again, his expense.

"It appears there are road washouts," said Zain. "It might be difficult getting into town.

"There may be ways of getting around the washouts."

"Let's hope," said Zain, but he wasn't holding much hope that that would be anytime soon.

"Hey, dad," came a call from back along the house. It was Erik jogging up in his gum boots. "Come look. All the animals found us. They're lined up in the stable and barn waiting to be fed."

"Oh boy," said Bo. "Only give them a quarter of what they normally get. They'll have to forage for the rest."

Turning to Zain, Bo said, "The pets are going to be on short rations too, if the road remains impassable for any time."

Zain and Bo returned to the kitchen, where Rose poured fresh coffee for them. Bo took his mug as he went out to check on the animals and try to figure out how to milk the cows.

"Elen says there's not very much wood left," said Rose. "Is there more stacked somewhere?"

"Yeah, there's more in the old carriage house, but that won't be enough. Get your cute pink rain gear. We'll get more."

Zain and Rose slogged through the driving rain to the stables. Zain fired up the antique, dropped the trailer, collected a choker cable and headed to the entry lane. Several of the old poplars had blown down. Those on the upwind side had fallen across the roadway.

"All these old, dead trees will have to be cleared before we can use the driveway. For now, we'll cut up this one for firewood before it gets too waterlogged."

Zain backed the tractor up to the butt section and hooked up the choker. Slowly, they chugged their way back up the hill. Rose ran ahead to open the front stable doors. Zain drove right in, dragging the tree into the shelter of the stables. With all the racket, a bunch of the Vasas' pets took flight for the barn.

Bo walked through the stables from the barn. "Hey, you've got six stanchions in the barn."

"What are stanchions?" asked Zain

Rose smirked. "I guess you're no farm boy."

"Afraid not."

Bo enlightened him. "That's the thing that holds the cow while its being milked. At least, we'll have a supply of milk."

"There are some old churns in one of the storerooms behind the kitchen," said Zain.

"Good, we can have fresh butter too."

Bo went on to the house. Zain picked up a chain saw in the studio and began cutting up the old tree.

"Where's an ax? I could use some exercise," said Rose.

"There's an ax and a splitting adz in the carriage house. Watch out, that adz will give you blisters in a hurry."

CHAPTER 5

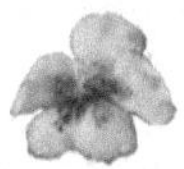

All through the day the storm raged. Darkness was abnormally early. After dinner the Vasas sat round the transistor radio waiting for another report on the dams upriver. The upper dam was leaking. If that dam water broke loose, it could sweep the Vasas house downriver. Concern was written on all their faces....even the five-year olds'.

Zain watched the preoccupation of the Vasas. He excused himself from the table and murmured to Rose as he went by that he was going to shower and shave before the horde arrived. He quietly mounted the stairs, dropped his clothes in the bedroom and stepped into the bathroom. He turned on the shower and while waiting for the hot water to arrive, he got a towel out of the cabinet. Although he would have liked to luxuriate under the hot water, he hastened his ablutions.

The shampoo was just starting down the drain when the Vasa kids' gathering cry sounded. Shaking the water from his eyes, he found Emil staring at his crotch.

Zain had lived for years in an art community where

modesty wasn't highly regarded. Also, Zain had done his share of nude modeling both for classes and privately. Of course, that was among adults....not kids. Under current legal dictates, an adult could hardly afford to look at a kid not his own. For that matter, photographing your own kid naked on a bear skin rug could get you in a peck of trouble. Now, he was standing stark naked in front of eight youngsters.

"Look, he's circumcised," announced Emil.

"Neat," declared Kas.

Zain decided he'd lost control of the situation, so he'd just roll with the action. He certainly didn't want to appear to be a prude. He finished rinsing and stepped out of the shower to dry.

Emil, the expert, was saying, "I told you, most of the guys at school are circumcised. They also call it 'cut'. Of course, all the Jewish boys look like that. It's some sort of religious thing."

Under such intense scrutiny, Zain was beginning to lose his physical composure.

"Hey," cried Elsa. "It looks like Pedro."

"Pedro?" said Zain.

"Yeah, Pedro's our burro. His *siitin* is always hanging out. Once-in-a-while, it gets hard and sticks out just like yours."

At that moment, the Vasa adults and Rose crowded into the bathroom. Rose was trying to stifle a giggle.

"Hey, what are you heathens up to now? Oh, for pity sakes, leave the poor man alone."

"Look, mom, look. He's circumcised. You said you'd never seen one before."

Carina began to turn red, but she said, "Scat. Quit pestering him. He's not used to a pack of marauding Vikings like you."

"Hey, dad, can Ken and I get circumcised?"

"We'll talk about that later. It's time for you young ones to get to sleep. Do as your mother says." The last statement took on an ominous tone. The two younger sets of twins fled to the parents' room.

"It's so long," said Inga, rather breathlessly, in what was supposed to be a whisper to her sister, which everyone heard.

"When you're six foot-two or so everything tends to get long," said Rose as she leaned against the door frame. She was enjoying herself.

Zain left the battlefield. He moved to the lavatory to shave. Apparently, Carina kept the kids at bay until he retreated to his bedroom.

Rose was in bed with the covers up to her waist. There wasn't any sense in covering up now, so Zain tossed his towel over a chair and climbed onto his side of the bed. He leaned against the headboard and pulled the covers up.

"Today was supposed to be a work day," said Rose.

"It didn't work out that way. It seems to me that we worked harder than we had planned."

"Are you going to be able to take your pictures?"

"Oh, I could take them with a flash, but that flattens everything so much, they are hard to use. We may be here a while. I hope you aren't on a tight schedule."

"No, not really. I have something I must do, but there is no time schedule."

"This storm should pass by tomorrow night, but the water will continue to rise until all the upstream runoff gets here. The dams may create more of a problem. In any case, we can't get out of here until the water recedes. Even then there may be a problem. It appears there are some road washouts."

"You won't have lights for a long time, will you?"

"No, I can see from here that some of the power poles are down. Those lines belong to me. I'll have to fix them.

Once the storm passes,we should have some nice sunny weather. I can shoot the photos outside in natural light.

"You can't do your work without electricity, can you?"

" I can't cast bronze without juice, but I can do modeling, mould making and then all sorts of brainless work such as cleaning up."

"Is sculpture all you do? What I mean is do you earn your living from art?"

"Almost. I teach that one class in life drawing. It brings in a little money, but I do it so I can keep track of the world outside. If I didn't do that or something like it, I'd bury myself out here and let the world go by. There is a small annuity that came with this place. It pays the taxes and regular upkeep. However, it won't cover the power lines and the road. I'll have to work out something else on that."

"You must be a pretty good sculptor to make your living out of it. Most of the artists I meet primarily teach for a living and occasionally sell something."

"Oh, I'm just beginning to build a reputation. It takes time to get known, but I'm working on it. I'm hoping that the bath towel series that I envision, will be a break-through work. I will be gunning for a one-man show in a major gallery."

"I hope you get it. Maybe, I'll be as famous as the model who was made famous by Picasso." Rose laughed and snuggled down under the covers.

Zain was aware of her watching him as he got up to turn out the lamp.

The next day was much like the preceding one. Everyone was awake at first light to check the water level on the Vasa house. It was not good. There were three feet of water in the ground floor. Bo was concerned that the structure might be swept away by the raging current.

Carina, Rose and the older girls prepared a lavish breakfast, using up the last of the perishable foods. Bo brought in a couple of pails of fresh milk. Zain was the only one without an assigned chore. He stayed out of the way by sitting at the kitchen table drinking coffee.

Carina took a break and sat down beside him. “Sorry about last night. None of the Vasa males are circumcised. When Erik and Emil got into a PE class where the boys had to dress down, they discovered something strange. It became a rather persistent topic of conversation. None of the other kids had ever seen one.”

“You too,” said Zain with a smirk.

Carina ducked her head and shuffled her feet a bit before answering. “Yeah, me too. Anyway, you presented an opportunity they couldn’t resist. I’m afraid you’ve had an influence on Kas and Ken. They are running around with their foreskins pulled back.”

Carina jumped up. “Inga, don’t let the pan smoke. Put it on the side.” Mom went back to work.

After breakfast Zain and Rose went back to splitting wood. The rain and the wind were backing off somewhat. Elsa burst in the side door, yelling, “Mom says come to the house.”

The family was grouped around the radio. “The upper dam just broke,” said Bo.

“Is it going to take out the next one?” asked Zain.

“They don’t know yet.”

Even the young ones realized this was an important event in their lives. The girls hung on to their mother and the boys sought comfort from their dad, who was there for them. The two older sets of twins sought strength from their twin.

Rose stood aside, paying more attention to the human drama unfolding before her than the reports of the fickle weather. This sort of interplay was new to her.

No more news concerning the dams was available so the gathering split up. Eventually, the whole Vasa family ended up on the front porch watching the dirty water swirl around their inundated house. A couple of small sheds floated away. The propane tank had broken loose and was bobbing around in the backwash of the house, spouting gas with every bobble.

A fresh squall drove the Vasas back indoors. The kids were restive. The morning chores were behind them. Now the twins were even beginning to snap at one another.

Zain yelled to Erik and Emil, "Get four lanterns from the store room." When they returned, Zain lit the lamps and said, "Okay everyone, come along."

Under the broad staircase to the second floor was a double door. Rose had noticed the door, but she assumed it was a closet. Actually, it was an entry to a staircase leading to a full basement. It was one big room..

"This is the game room," said Zain. "When I say game, I actually mean deer, elk, pheasant or whatever the hunters brought in. See the steel rail hanging from the ceiling with all the hooks? That's for hanging deer while cleaning them."

"Cleaning?" asked Elsa.

"Gutting. Like when we butcher pigs." said Inga.

"Look at that fireplace," exclaimed Erik. "I could stand in it."

"See that chain come-along? They used to drag whole logs into that fireplace. When they weren't butchering game, this was a party and play room. There's shuffle board, pool and billiard tables, darts, poker tables down at the other end of the room. All the equipment is in the cabinets along the wall."

Zain thought he was going to turn the kids loose, but that didn't work. He ended up giving lessons on how to play and score each of the games. None had ever seen them played before.

Rose dropped in to see what was happening. After the

instruction sessions, she rescued him from the challenges of the kids.

"What are you doing to the psyches of those poor, sweet kids? First it's circumcision, and now it pool hall games. I think there's trouble in River City."

Zain shrugged. "If you're raised on a farm, you'll grow up to be a pumpkin seed. As long as you stay on the farm, that's all right. But if you stray off the farm, you're in trouble. Look at all the fun they had at my expense because I didn't know what a stanchion was."

By noon they had the word. All three of the earthen dams had ruptured. A wall of muddy water was making its way down the valley. There were no further reports since the dams were located in a remote, virtually unpopulated area. By the time the water got down to civilization, the valley would widen enough so only minimal effects would be felt. However, at their position along that route, the Vasa house was in danger.

There was one attenuating factor. The water had risen far enough that the promontory where Zain's house sat had come into play. It was forming a screen for the Vasa house. The water would rise around the house, but the ever increasing volume of debris was being deflected away.

Bo and Carina let the kids play a couple of hours before sending them back to work. Dinner was a very staple-oriented meal. Carina had only dry and canned goods at her disposal, but she just about drove everyone wild with the aroma of fresh baked bread. The hot bread with fresh churned butter was the high point of the day as far as Zain was concerned. Rose was also profuse in her expressions of appreciation.

Without lights, everyone headed for bed just after the dishes were finished.

"After this is all done, you're going to have some pretty big expenses," said Rose, as she waited for the bathroom traffic to subside.

"Yeah. So far there hasn't been any appreciable damage to the house. There are some shingles off the barn, but I think I can tack in a few new ones."

"How about the electrical?"

"That and the road will be a problem. And then there may be another factor. When those three earthen dams went that meant tons and tons of mud was added to the mix. This whole valley may be one big mud pie and when it dries it will be as solid as concrete with a lot of big cracks. It may be a long time before there will be any stock grazing.

"Oh, boy. What will Bo do?"

"He may have to pick up and leave. It's going to cost him a lot to get straightened out. The whole house will need work to become liveable. He'll have well problems, for a long time. He'll probably need a new pump. If ground water got in, it will be contaminated until he can purify and pump it clean."

"How are you going to pay for all your repairs? It could be a staggering amount when you add up the electrical service and now a new road?"

"As I said, there's a little money set aside for repairs. A lot of the stuff I can do myself. There's a stand of pole pine up behind us. I'll cut the poles and haul them down with the tractor. I hope I can salvage much of the wire. I have a power auger to set the poles. When I run out of money, I'll just have sell some sculpture."

"Can't you get some sort of government aide?"

"I've never inquired. It's my problem, not someone else's."

"That's why they set up aid programs....to help people."

"Oh, I could never charge someone else to pay for my problem. I'll accept help from Bo because he'll derive a benefit, but there's no benefit to the taxpayer."

Rose shook her head. Muttering more to herself than

Zain, she said, “If it’s there, why not use it?” as she headed for the bathroom.

That night Zain found sleep elusive. As he teetered on the edge of the bed, he kept thinking about the strange female on the other side. She was very attractive., She’ll make a marvelous model, if she can hold a pose. He could become interested in her, but there was more than physical considerations in his book. He’d always maintained a qualifying list of attributes that had to be met before he would consider any entangling alliances. The list changed from time to time as he grew older and acquired a more mature perspective on life.

Tattooing was not on his list because it never had occurred to him that body mutilation would be one of the judging factors on a female.

On a guy, tattoos would not be a rejection factor for friendship, but their presence would lower the wearer in his overall estimation.

Zain rather liked Rose’s sense of freedom. He wondered if that freedom came from her adroit management of “the system.” In college there were kids who could find either a government agency or a charitable group that would provide almost anything they needed or wanted, even though they could well afford to pay for it themselves. It was a big game.

Besides her looks, he found her empathy attractive. Of course, his skepticism surfaced, telling him that it was easy to pay lip service to all sorts of pitiful human conditions and causes. Liberals made their living doing that.

Just before he finally dropped off to sleep, Zain began to wonder about Rose’s tattoo. He’d had several glimpses of it from a distance under dim lantern light or the first rays of a new day that were filtered by window shades. He’d never been able to distinguish what it represented. The only pictures of solid tattooed areas he’d seen were from

Japan where there were people with full body disfiguration. Rose's didn't seem to have a dominant theme such as the Japanese Samurai surrounded by battle scenes. He decided he'd have to get a close look. As soon as he got some decent, dry daylight, he'd set up a modeling session. When he measured her, he'd have a legitimate reason for getting up close and personal.

On the other side of the bed, Rose was going through her own mental gymnastics. The guy across from her was balanced on the edge of the bed as if he wanted to get as far away from her as possible. She wondered if he's queer. That would really be a waste. He's tall and attractive. He has the "all male" look, but she'd found that could be deceiving.

Maybe it was she that he found objectionable. Maybe he liked his women with big boobs. He said he liked her figure for his sculpture, but that may have been a commercial consideration rather than a personal one.

He's so straight. Maybe he was brought up in one of those strict pentecostal churches. But, he drinks beer.

CHAPTER 6

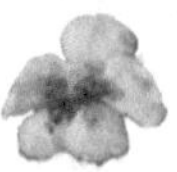

By morning, the storm had abated. The wind dropped to a stiff breeze. There was no rain. The whole world was saturated. Any bare ground had turned to mud. Boots became caked with great gobs of sticky earth. Kas and Ken were given the job of cleaning the mud off the boots in the mud room.

Breakfast was chunks of homemade bread in hot milk. That was a new experience for Zain, but it appeared to be common fare for the Vasas.

Although the rains had stopped, the river was still rising. Everyone was keeping an eye on the water level because the dam water could arrive at anytime.

It arrived in the middle of breakfast. There was an audible murmur when the front wall arrived. The Vasa family stood arm-in-arm as their house sunk deeper into the swirling, muddy water.

Bo let out a long sigh. "I was afraid there would be a big wall of water. It was only six inches or so high. We're lucky."

Lucky meant that the water only got a few inches deep on

the second floor. The rest of the house was up to the eaves. Most of the little farm sheds floated away.

With the dam water came tons of debris. Uprooted trees locked horns with old snags forming a great twisting, turning mass. Zain's entry road deflected the current and its load of debris away from the Vasa buildings. The debris did rip out all of their fencing.

Day-by-day the Vasa family lost more and more of their physical worth. Bo was looking more grim each day. It was up to Carina to handle the kids and to keep them from worrying excessively about their future. She spent considerable thought devising diversions.

One such diversion came just after lunch. Carina took Rose aside to confer on something. Such an action in an open family immediately sent up all the kids' antennae. Rose agreed to something with a nod of the head.

Carina called Inga, Inger, Elen and Elsa. "Come with us." Rose and Carina led the way out into the hall heading for the stairs. The other twins started to follow along, but they were cut short. "Stay here, this is a girl thing."

There had never been girl things and boy things before. The boys stood in silence, following the females with their ears. When the bathroom door closed with a loud thump, the boys tumbled over each other getting to a position under the bathroom. They couldn't distinguish anything from that point. Emil tried to sneak up the stairs. Bo cut that off. "You heard what your mother said. Get back in here....all of you." To make things worse, Bo decided he needed help in the barn and herded his male heirs out of the house.

Left alone, Zain started cleaning up the rest of the kitchen clutter. His curiosity was aroused, but he wouldn't let it show. While alone, he went into the pantry to assess the food supply. There wasn't much besides staples. They could keep from going hungry for a few days but he doubted if they would be able to get through the valley before the food ran out.

He sorely missed his computer. All his financial information was in it. Through it he could access his bank accounts. Also he could call up maps of his surrounding areas. In the absence of the computer, he would have to conduct his research the old fashioned way....from books and maps.

Zain thumped up the stairs and banged his way into his bedroom/study. From a drawer he pulled out copies of county land maps of the estate and various other maps that had come with the inheritance. He was looking for an upland route into a populated area. He might have to cross any number of properties. There were a couple of possible routes depending on the lay-of-the-land. He wished for topographic maps, which he could have gotten off the net....but alas.

When all the girls trooped downstairs, they wore smug looks. Zain got Rose aside, “Well, what was that all about?”

Rose just smiled. “I don’t want to to spoil Carina’s party. You’ll see in due course. How are the boys taking their exclusion?”

“Not well. They are about to chew on their left ankles. This must have been a first.”

Rose smiled again as she headed for the kitchen.

Zain intervened. “If you’re not required to be elsewhere, I could use a little help.”

“Sure, I can help. What are we up to?”

“I’m going to put a second seat on the tractor. If I had electricity, it would be a simple task with the electric welder. Now I’ll have to use oxygen/acetylene. I’ll need someone to hold the pieces as I weld.”

“Why do you need as second seat?”

“This water isn’t going down soon and when it does, the road will probably be impassable for a while. We’re going to run out of food soon. The livestock is already trying to survive on forage, which is scarce. Our only source of food will be the kids' pets."

"Oh, no. We can't do that!"

"There is no sense in butchering one of the large critters. Most of the meat would spoil before we could eat it. So, I'm going across the high country to get supplies. I'll take one person with me, so I'll need another seat. I'll also build a box on the trailer to carry extra fuel, trailer tires, tools, chain saw.....supplies"

"Who's going with you?"

"Don't know yet."

"How long's your little trip going to take?"

"Hard to tell. The old lady only goes about two and a half miles an hour on a slightly downhill grade. If there aren't too many detours, it's about nine or ten miles to a major road. There's no sense in trying for our little county road. It's probably out too. When we hit the main road, we'll have to hitchhike into town. I can't drive the tractor on the roads. It would chew them up and I'd have to pay some big fines. There's another route that would take us closer to town, but it's considerably longer and steeper. Of course, if there are washouts, canyons, whatnot, I might not be able to get the tractor through. That would mean a long walk."

"I'm the logical one to go with you."

"How did you come to that conclusion?"

"Bo would be the best, but I don't think both men should leave the women folk and kids to fend for themselves. Carina is needed here to take care of the kids. Erik and Emil are too young and not experienced enough to know what to do in an emergency. Besides, kids have a lot of short term energy, but it flags over the long haul. I've never driven the tractor, but I could do it since I watched you when we picked up the Vasas. I'm stronger than the boys and I can probably out-walk you. And I know how to hitchhike. How many times have you ever hitched a ride?"

"Okay, okay. You've made your case. I was hoping you'd see it that way."

"Oh, you bastard," said Rose with a good-natured laugh. "When are we gong on this safari?"

"It has to dry out a little bit....in a couple/three days.... providing we don't get another storm. That will give us time to get a modeling session in. I'm going to pull the stand outside to use natural light. All right?"

"Sure, that's fine with me."

Zain and Rose spent the rest of the daylight adding the new seat and constructing a box on the trailer.

At last light, Inga announced that the water level was falling. She had spotted the dirty high-water mark on the house above the swirling waters. Everyone walked down to water's edge to get a closer look. Yep, it was getting lower.

After dinner, the little kids were sent off to bed. The adults and the older boys were lingering over their coffee discussing Zain's plan to tractor out for food. Bo didn't like being left behind, but logic was against him and most of his life had rested on the rule of logic. He finally said he'd would give Zain a letter to the Johnson Feed and Seed where he had a line of credit. That should cover all the stock feed the trailer could carry.

I don't imagine I can put together more than eighty dollars in cash," said Bo. "I've got another three hundred in my checking account. I'll give you a check to pay for groceries."

"I'll put it on my credit card and we can settle up later. Carina, I want you to make a shopping list to keep us going for at least two weeks. Include anything else we need such as toiletries and the like."

Their deliberations were interrupted by a great roar from the bathroom. It was followed by the gathering call. Erik and Emil made quick, unexcused departures. Bo and Zain looked questioningly at each other. Rose and Carina started their descent in hysterical laughter.

Bo started for the stairs. Carina, through her laughter, yelled, "Come back here. Let them have their fun."

"What fun?"

"This afternoon Rose showed the girls....and me....how to use the bidets."

"The whats?"

"The bidets. Those porcelain things next to the toilets. Rose says it's French. Anyway, I suspect that the girls started to use them in front of Ken and Kas. This should break up some of the mopery that's been building around here."

Later, when Rose and Zain headed for bed, Rose was still grinning over the bidet affair. Changing to a more pressing matter, Rose said, "We've gone through a mountain of pink and green bath towels. Everyone is getting a little whiffy. We need to do some wash. Have you any ideas?"

"Go out the back door, behind the kitchen. To the left of the carriage house is the old wash house. I looked in when I first came up to look at the place. There's a wood stove and tubs. I think they used to boil their clothes. Oh, yes, there is a crank wringer. There used to be clothes lines behind. If not, I can restring them. Oh, yes, there are lines in the basement that can be stretched when needed."

"I'll take a look tomorrow."

"Don't forget, tomorrow is a work day. I'd like to start about 10:00, when the sun is at a good angle."

There was a scratching at the door. "That sounds like Wolf. I wonder what's wrong," said Zain as he slid out of bed.

"I imagine he's lonely. He's been getting short shrift since the Vasas moved in. You dump some food in his dish once a day and give him a perfunctory pat on the head. I'd guess he's used to more."

When Zain opened the door, Wolf came bounding in with his tail wagging violently. Nutsy also made an entry in a much more dignified manner, with his tail straight in the air.

Zain sat down in the middle of the floor to roughhouse with Wolf, who luxuriated in the attention.

Nutsy went on a sniff-sniff tour of the room concentrating on Rose's backpack, boots and jeans that were draped over the chair. Apparently, whatever criterion was in play was satisfied. He jumped onto the bed and laid down next to Rose's thigh and slowly wrapped his long tail around his body.

Zain pulled Wolf down on the floor and gathered his legs together. Then he leaned over the dog and bit Wolf's cheek. When he was released, Wolf rolled over on his back and wagged his tail.

"What are you doing?" said Rose.

"In dog language, I'm telling him who's top dog around here."

"You speak 'dog'?" said Rose with a chuckle.

"That much I do. He's happy knowing where he stands."

What good does that do?"

"One benefit is that I don't have to smell him all the time. Now he doesn't have to go around peeing on everything to stake out his territory."

"Now, I suppose you have to pee on everything." Rose was stroking a contented cat who had his motor going.

"These guys aren't supposed to be in the bedroom."

"There isn't supposed to be a houseful of strangers diverting your attention from your buddies either. Let 'em stay."

"Well, okay. I suppose I'll pay for this down the line. Don't complain to me if you get chewed up by fleas."

Early the next morning, Zain put a clean memory stick in his digital camera and hiked along the high ground so he could get a sunrise shot of the east side of the Vasa house. The high water mark showed clearly. The artist in him prevented his taking casual shots. His photos had to be composed with the maximum amount of drama possible. As the day progressed, he caught various members of the Vasa family going about their day. Carina was stirring a big kettle of oatmeal on the wood-burning cook stove. Elsa was hugging her Pot Bellied pig. He caught Kas trudging through the muddy yard with a flock of hungry geese, ducks, peafowl and guinea hens trailing behind. Actually, the dramatic shot was of the long shadow they cast with the early morning sun.

He went through the whole family individually and then he composed a group shot around the old tractor. A wide shot showed both the tractor and trailer. At no time did he show his own house other than bits such as the wood stove.

Rose had been watching the process. "What are all those pictures for?"

"Just think if I came into your feed store and I was trying to get merchandise on someone else's credit account. Would you believe me? You have to admit it would sound pretty far fetched. These will back up our story."

After the photo session, Zain borrowed Erik and Emil to help him move the model stand outside to a level, grassy patch of ground. He changed his memory stick and called Rose to work.

While she was stripping, Zain made a quick sketch of the frontal view of a figure in a spiral notebook.

"I need accurate measurements of your entire body."

"Go ahead."

Zain began the process with his normal professional detachment. Height could wait until he could use the scale on the wall of the studio. With a cloth tape, he measured the circumference of the head and neck....the length of the face. The figures were recorded on the sketch. He went down the body making similar measurements until he came face to face with the tattoo.

"Oh, they're roses.," Zain exclaimed.

"Wild roses," said Rose in a tone that indicated that he was somewhere below normal...not making proper distinction.

"Yes, wild roses, pink wild roses," said Zain and felt foolish for saying it. He sounded like a junior high school kid. The roses were beautifully executed...But they were tattoos

As Zain continued his measurements, he was obliged to touch the mutilated skin. He was surprised to find it was as smooth as all of Rose's skin. He didn't know what to expect but he felt it must be different.

Rose stood perfectly still with her own professional detachment. She was disappointed in Zain's reaction to her beautiful tattoo. He'd summarily dismissed her creative efforts with an inane comment, "Oh, it's roses." She'd expected something more from an artist.

When the measurements were duly recorded on the sketch, Zain had her stand facing him with her feet about eight inches apart and her arms hanging straight down. He took the first picture. Then he moved around the model to get a profile and a back shot.

The actual modelling session began with the pose depicting a dejected loser with a towel around the neck and stretched tight by a grip on the ends. The head was bowed. Zain fussed over the pose until he had what he wanted. Then he used an adjustable monopod so that each shot would be taken at navel level. Exposures were taken from each of the cardinal direction. Next he abandoned the monopod to take details of the head, hands, feet and what ever else was not completely explained in the earlier photos.

The whole pose took only three minutes before they moved into another set-up. Usually she sat or stood for hours in the same position at twenty minutes on and five minutes off. This was an easy way to make money. Zain had a list of poses he wanted to investigate. As soon as he was satisfied with the balance, gesture and attitude from all directions, Rose froze in the position until the photos were taken.

Both Erik and Emil remained to watch the proceedings. They were fascinated by the process. Normally, Zain would have surmised that a couple of thirteen-year-olds would have been ogling the naked lady, but that didn't seem to be the case.

After an hour of continuous work, Zain said, "Let's call it quits for the day. I surely wish I had my computer so I could see how these are coming out. Tomorrow, we'll have another session. I have to rethink some of these poses, and others have occurred to me as we were working today."

Rose stretched, more for effect than through necessity. "You have all the information you need out of those photographs?"

"Yep."

"I don't understand."

"I'll make prints of all the shots of each pose plus the front, back and side shots. On the back shot, I'll draw a stick figure with a line from the top of the head to the tail bone. Two other lines go across the shoulders to the shoulder joint and the hips to the leg joint. Lines go down the center of the arms and the legs. Say the photograph of the figure is ten inches high. If I want to sculpt a figure fifty inches high, I multiply each of the lines on the figure by five to get the measurements for the figure. I use those numbers to build a steel armature. That way all parts of the body are proportional. It takes much of the guesswork out of the process.

"Tomorrow I'll have some poses that will have much more action in them. You'd never be able to hold them long enough for me to directly work from the model."

Zain didn't have to go far to find the twins to help him return the model stand to the studio. They had been parked practically in his hind pocket as he was explaining the procedure to Rose, taking the measurements and shooting the photos.

That night as Wolf and Nutsy were getting their evening dose of affection, Rose commented, "I haven't seen any examples of your work. Do you have anything around the house?"

"Not right now. When you're trying to make a living out of art, things change from when you had a day job. You can't sell a piece until it's completely finished. I hate to make bases, but it's part of the process of getting the work ready for the market. As soon as I get a final patina on a bronze, I clench my teeth until I get a proper base on the piece.

"When I lived in town I had any number of pieces at home. I've always sold most of my work, but since I moved out here I only occasionally get a client out this far from town. They seem to think I live two countries away. Now, as soon as a piece is complete it goes out to a gallery.

"There are several pieces in various stages of completion, but they are in humidity boxes in the studio. Without lights, they are hard to see. There are more pieces in molds, ready to cast as soon as we get some juice."

Zain went to his computer desk. From a book shelf he pulled a large magnetic-paged photo album. "If you want to see a chronology, start at the back. The latest pieces are on the top page."

He was never comfortable when someone was going through his creative history. Those early pieces weren't very good....lousy was a better term. Zain wandered off to the bathroom to brush his teeth so as to avoid some of the inane comments that usually accompanied the scrutinizing of his album.

After dawdling as long a possible, Zain returned to the

bedroom. Rose had moved to his desk to be closer to a lamp. She had started from the rear, but she was holding places with fingers. "What are the symbols you use? Do the gold dots indicate sales?"

"Yeah."

"What about the red dot with the 'C'?"

"C is for cannibalized. I tore It apart and used parts on other pieces or, if it was bronze, it went back in the pot. The original wasn't very good."

"S?"

"Stolen."

"Stolen? Does that happen very often?"

"When I first started trying to sell, I had to put stuff anywhere I could get exposure. That meant restaurants, book stores, public office spaces....you name it. This is how you build a resumé. As you get better and more widely known you can rate better places. But until you get into the better galleries, you don't have any security from theft and damage insurance. It doesn't happen very often now."

"You've gone through several stages. Are these first ones assemblages?"

"Yeah, that and found art, junk art and 'you've got to be kidding art'. That's the easiest to do. It doesn't take very many tools."

"You went through a long period of carving."

"Again, the materials are cheap and you can make do with only a few tools. Of course, if you want, you can also tie up a fortune in good woodcarving tools."

"Now you do bronzes."

"I've always like additive sculpture, but it takes a while to be able to afford it. The materials are expensive. You need a lot of space and costly equipment. I'm still working toward a state where I can sculpt and turn the clay over to someone else and the next time I see the piece, it will be a finished bronze on a base ready to take to a gallery. That's still a long way off."

The question and answer session went well into the night. Wolf and Nutsy gave up and went to sleep. The Vasas had long since gone to their slumbers.

The next morning, Carina dispatched Kas and Ken to chase each other up and down the stairs and through the hallways so Zain and Rose wouldn't miss breakfast.

When the sun was at the proper angle, Zain was ready to start the next photo session. Erik and Emil were ready assistants and interested spectators. As Zain had promised, the poses involved a lot of action. Several positions required Rose to rise up on the ball of one foot while kicking or prancing. She had to repeat the action time and time again as Zain took his photos from the various sides and angles.

Rose had never posed in that manner before, but she quickly recognized Zain's intentions and easily fell into the routine. As in the first session, the towel was always involved in some way.

When Zain had gone through all of his planned poses, he gave Rose a rest while he noted other actions that had occurred to him during the preceding session. Also, he listed improvements on some of the poses he had already done.

"I don't like figurative sculpture that just looks like a lump that has grown roots. A sculpture can't move, so I like to add at least the implication of motion. The viewer then gets the feeling that the figure is about to take a step or jump. It no longer looks static."

"Where did you learn this?

"I came up with it myself. That was the subject of my MFA thesis...'The Use of Action Photography in Figurative Sculpture'."

"I'd like to see those pictures."

"Me too, but until we get electricity, I can't put them

into the computer. I can show you a few if we step into the studio where there is less light. I have to be careful I don't use up my batteries until I can get more. I have some rechargeable ones but I can't charge them now."

CHAPTER 7

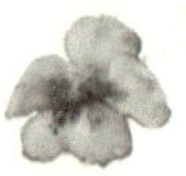

At first light, Zain cranked up the tractor. The whole Vasa family was lined up on the porch for the sendoff. Zain plopped down in the driver's seat. Rose was already in the rumbleseat. Zain adjusted the magnito and slowly the mighty Titan pulled away. The three days of sunshine had done a lot to firm up the high ground. In the valley, the water had receded so it covered only half of the first floor.

The journey was slow and tedious. Zain cut the fence at the edge of his property and delayed long enough to make a gate as Bo had done. Beyond the fence, the land had been grazed in recent years. It was clear enough to avoid various hazards such as rock outcroppings, washouts and sloping land.

The ride was rough. Every jolt went straight up the spine and tried to snap their heads off. Conversation was restricted to an occasional shout above the roar of the tractor. Rose tried to hang onto the rounded edge of Zain's steel seat but when the going got tough, she had to lean forward and grab him around the waist.

Zain was acutely aware of the arms around his middle, but he tried not to dwell on it. He was afraid he would involuntarily embarrass himself.

Rose was fighting her own battle with the hump in her contoured seat.

They cut their way through two more fences. The sun passed its zenith before Zain motioned ahead and shouted, "Aspen Mountain Road. Our road runs into it. It should still be open. It crosses the Conchero. That's the little river that goes by my place."

"Which way's town?"

"To the right, but as I recall there's a house further up the hill. We're going to turn left."

Zain swung the tractor to the left and started to chug up the hill. The road was in a deep cut below them. Rose stood to relieve her posterior. Her hands on Zain shoulders gripped harder as she shouted, "There it is."

Moments later, as the tractor crowned the hill, a gentleman's farm came into Zain's view. There was a cluster of immaculate buildings surrounded by white rail fences.

"We'll see if we can leave the tractor here and hitchhike into town." Zain made a broad swing so he could pull the tractor and trailer parallel to the fence. He turned off the engine with the remark, "Boy, that silence sounds good."

A little boy had been watching from a corner of the house. When Zain and Rose dismounted, the kid ran for the back door yelling, "Mom, Mom."

The curtain, in what was probably the kitchen, was already fluttering. That wasn't surprising, since their approach had been anything but silent. Zain pulled Rose's backpack and his sports bag from the trailer box.

When the pair vaulted over the fence, the lady of the house took up a position in the open back door. The little boy was peering around her leg. She was obviously pregnant.

Zain advanced with a broad smile. With still a substantial safety distance between them Zain said, "Good afternoon, ma'am. I'm Zain Zook and this is my friend Rose. I have the old Graff place up the river. We, along with Vasa family are stranded up the valley. Rose and I are on a supply run. We're running out of food and animal fodder."

"Is everyone all right?"

"The water is up to the second floor on the Vasa house, but everyone is all right. The family is staying with us. The road is washed out and the power lines are down, but we're doing fine. We're running short of food and we've got a bunch of hungry critters following us around.

"We had to cut your fence to get here. We put a gate in it so we can get back through, but no stock can get out."

"I'm Judge Raymond Winter's wife, Pamela, I'm so sorry to hear of your problems. What can I do?"

"If you'll let us park the tractor there, we'll hitchhike into town. In a couple of days we should be able to truck our supplies out, load the trailer and move that ugly contraption out of your yard."

"Oh, don't worry about the tractor. It won't bother anyone. Let me get my keys. I'll drive you into town."

"You don't have to bother," said Rose. "We can make it into town."

"I wouldn't feel right letting you hitchhike. I'd rather take you. Girls shouldn't have to stick out their thumbs."

Zain and Rose exchanged small smiles.

Twenty minutes later, Pamela Winters headed her SUV toward town. "Where do you want to go?"

"We need a reasonable motel in close to the business district," said Zain. "We can use the motel as a base of operations. We need to rent a pickup to haul things around."

"Do what you have to do. Don't worry about the tractor. We'll watch over it. If you need to store things until you're ready to leave, you can use one of our garages."

Mrs. Winters dropped them off at the office of the Continental. After they had registered and they were lugging their duffle to the room, Rose said, "Why don't we rent a big truck. We can lock our stuff in there until we're ready to leave."

"Good idea. That will solve a lot of problems. Let's dump these bags and get down to the Walgreens a few blocks down the street. I want to have these photos tomorrow. There's a U-Haul on past the drug store. Can you delay dinner until we get back?"

"No problem. Could we get two prints per photo? I have a little idea floating around."

"I suppose so. What do you have in mind?"

"Let me think on it for a bit more before I try to explain it."

The photos turned out to be everything Zain had hoped. They had the artistic drama and imbalance that suggested action such as he always tried to incorporate into his sculpture. Rose was delighted with them all, but especially the ones with Kas and the fowl.

They had to hustle to get to the truck rental place before it closed. They rented one big enough to haul all they would be able to get on the trailer.

After dinner they stopped by the bar for a couple of beers before retiring to their room. Zain had asked for two beds. He flopped down on one. Instead of taking up residence on the other, Rose claimed the desk and telephone. Rummaging through the desk, she found writing paper, a pen and the phone book.

"What are you up to?" asked Zain.

"I'm trying to find out if I have a viable idea."

Rose dialed a number she'd extracted from the phone book. "Would you please tell me who is in charge of the flood coverage?"

"Umm....How do you spell it?...Is he in?....I have something he should like."

There was a pause. "Mr. Hawk? My name is Rose. I have

before me a set of absolutely wonderful photos a friend took of a family, composed of four sets of twins, who is stranded up the Conchero River. They're running low on food and animal fodder. My friend and I have driven an antique tractor through the mountains on a mission of mercy since the road is washed out."

Zain rolled his eyes toward the ceiling and started to object, but he was silenced with a motion of her hand as Rose launched her pitch.

"Before we even get to the flood, have you ever heard of a family with four sets of twins? That's a study in itself. Then add to it a whole entourage of pets, a Pot Bellied pig, a burro, Guinea hens, peahens, muscovies, rabbits, goats, funny-looking chickens, geese with top knots, horses, pony and a herd of cattle....all stranded without the necessities of life. The first floor of their house is underwater as is the barn. The outbuildings have floated away. I've got wonderful photos of all this. Are you interested in seeing them?"

"Good. We're at the Continental, room twelve. We'll be waiting. If you hurry, you can make the 10:00 o'clock news." Rose was smiling as she hung up. "He's hooked."

"What's all this about?"

"The Vasas are facing financial ruin. There's help out there if you can get the word out. Bo's so straight he wouldn't go looking for it."

"You talk to Bo about this?"

"No. I didn't think about this until my butt was so sore from that tractor seat that I had to think about something else. I'll have to check. I think my roses may have wilted. Besides, if I'd thought of it before I left, I'd never have mentioned it to Bo. He'd have objected."

"Since he's not here, he can't say no."

Rose smiled sweetly. "These programs are set up for situations just like this. The only difference this time is that the Vasas really need some help where most of the money is given to people who fake their plight. Bo may be willing to go it alone, but what of all those kids? Why should they be deprived of things they need while Bo rebuilds the ranch?"

"Where is this going to go?"

"I have no idea. We'll get a little publicity first and see what develops."

Zain still wasn't convinced that disaster wasn't just around the corner by the time Hunter Hawk arrived at the door. The young Channel Six reporter, who had hair fit for a prime-time news anchorman....and he knew it.... blew into the room, followed by his cameraman. He made a valiant attempt to fill the entire space with his presence by alternately engaging in introductions and ordering his cameraman around.

Zain was inclined to let him blow, but it became apparent that Rose wasn't going to relinquish the stage. She pulled out the straight backed chair from the desk.

"First, sit down so you can see these marvelous pictures." She gently pushed him into the seat as she leaned across to lay out the photos, one by one. The first shot was of the submerged house and farm yard.

"Can you imagine the heartache this family had as they watched the water level creep up the walls?" She laid down the family portrait where the twins were paired up. "Ten lives have just gone down the river."

Rose went through each of the photos giving a brief explanation. Every time she reached out with a new print, she leaned across his line of sight exuding great gobs of sexuality. The poor reporter didn't have a chance.

Zain was having difficulty keeping a smirk off his face. He glanced at the photographer who was having an even worse time controlling his facial expressions.

The session ended with Hawk conducting an interview which featured Rose standing in front of the rental truck.

Rose explained the plight of the Vasa family. Due to time constraints, she could only introduce three photos....the flooded house, the family in front of the old tractor and trailer and Kas with the trailing hungry farm animals.

Rose concluded by making an appeal. "These folks could certainly use a little help. They currently are staying with a neighbor, who is also stranded. They have shelter and clothes but the food is running out, as well as fodder for the animals. Our valiant reporter Hunter Hawk would be the best to coordinate any relief effort on behalf of Mr. and Mrs. Vasa and their four sets of twins. You can do that, can't you Hunter?"

The camera swung back to Hawk, who had enough presence to not miss a beat. "Certainly. Anyone wishing to help can reach me at Channel Six." He gave the phone number before signing off.

Hawk quickly packed up and headed back to the studio to meet a deadline.

Zain and Rose adjourned to the bar for a beer. Zain wasn't particularly sanguine about the TV coverage, but Rose hadn't made any outlandish requests. All she did was appeal for help from anyone who cared to participate. Rose and Zain were too tired to dawdle long. They returned to their room to watch the late news, but both fell asleep before the segment aired.

Morning arrived with the insistent ringing of the phone. Rose made it to the phone first. Zain rolled over to look at his watch, which indicated it was 6:00 am.

"Oh, Hunter, what are you doing up so early?"

Hunter intoned into Rose's ear, "It's not early....it's late. I'm still at the station because of your little plea for help. That kid and all those damned geese is what did it."

"Did what? What are you talking about?"

"Your bit was at the end of the newscast. Nearly everyone had left the studio when Ed Swanson, of Swanson Feed and Seed, the place where Bo Vasa buys his feed, called to donate a ton of hay and enough feed to carry your critters through the crisis.

"Then the head of Emergency Management called wanting to know about your case. He knows he is going to have to field a bunch of question on how such a family fell through the cracks. Then PETA called accusing the station of cruelty to animals because we have a helicopter and we haven't sent a relief flight out there. Guess who the manager called?

"Then the contribution calls started coming in. Everyone else left and I've been on the phones all night. And now the boss wants a follow-up story. I'll never get any sleep."

"My, how wonderful. I knew you could light some fires. It will really help that poor family." Rose's voice dropped to a conspiratorial level. "Don't forget to gather some publicity for yourself. A person with your talents and looks shouldn't have to stay long in this small market."

Hawk suddenly lost a lot of his petulance and got back to business. "As soon as our helicopter gets off the morning traffic report at 9:00, I'm going to fly up the river to the ruptured dams and then I'm going to drop in on the Vasa family for a little visit to give them the word that help is on the way."

Rose said, "Just a moment." She clamped the speaker against her rose-cover hip. "Help is rolling in for Bo and Carina. The reporter is going to helicopter up to tell them and get a follow-up story."

Zain took a deep breath and puffed out his cheeks as he exhaled. "You'd better go with him to explain to Bo or tell that reporter to wear a flack jacket."

"Really?" said Rose as she tried to figure out why anyone would object to a little assistance in a crisis.

"You're making nasty implications concerning Bo's manhood and his ability to care for his family."

Quickly, Rose got back on the phone. "I think it might be a good idea if I went with you. The husband is very much a rugged independent. If you don't want a confrontation that might ruin all your good work, you better let me explain the situation to him first."

"Can you call him?" asked Hawk.

"The flood took out both the power and phone."

"It'll be tight. I'll pick you up at 9:15. Be ready." Hawk hung up.

Zain figured his night was over, so he sat cross-legged on his bed awaiting a report.

Rose detoured by the bathroom and then took up a similar position on her bed.

"What's going on?"

Rose was pleased with herself. She launched into a glowing report of the various factors at work. Zain listened, but he expressed no enthusiasm over her list of players and her speculation of how they might become involved.

She couldn't understand Zain's reticence in expressing pleasure. All sorts of wonderful things were developing.... free. For the proper cause, businesses and people always lined up to get a piece of a worthy endeavor....it made them feel good to help someone whom they viewed as less fortunate or a victim of forces beyond his control. The Vasas have all the elements of a great story.

Of course, many of those bleeding hearts had ulterior motives. Swanson would elevate his humanitarianism standing in this small town, get a nice tax deduction and a heap of free publicity he could never buy. Everyone wins. Even Rose would benefit. There wasn't anything she really wanted, but she would derive an inner satisfaction that would make her feel good about herself for a long time. She had mattered.

Zain mentally shrugged at Rose's raging speculation of all the freebies that were in the pipeline for the Vasas. He headed for the shower. There was a long day ahead for him.

After a quick breakfast, Zain left Rose at the motel to wait for Hawk. He started his rounds by going to his bank to juggle money around so he'd have enough available for the job ahead.

All morning, Zain systematically went down his shopping list. The truck swallowed up his purchases because he was working on specialty items such as hygienic supplies. He would have gone for the feed store first thing, but it seemed sensible to wait until the contribution game played out.

At noon, he checked with the motel. Rose hadn't returned. Since he had the truck parked, he stopped by the restaurant for lunch. Rose and Hunter found him rearranging the shopping lists.

Rose slid into the booth with a "Hi."

Hawk plopped down beside her. He started the conversation with, "What a whoppin' big house you've got. That's some place. Some people have all the luck."

"I'm lucky until next spring when I have to paint that big hulk. Do you want to help?" said Zain a little sourly. He was beginning to take a dislike to this guy. He reminded Zain of a false-front building. Zain knew the street-side was fake but so far he didn't know what was lurking behind.

Rose ignored the exchange, as she launched into an animated report of all the new developments. "Since the area has been designated a disaster area, FEMA and the SBA are in play. Both you and Bo should qualify for some of their programs. I know where to pick up the forms since you can't register by phone.

"This morning there have been several more major contributors. Food Pantry has donated a $500 shopping spree in one of their stores. Kaiser Lumber company has come through with $1000 in building supplies when Bo starts redoing his house.

"Oh yes, Disaster Management has arranged for a large National Guard helicopter to fly a load of supplies in tomorrow morning. Isn't that exciting?"

"You've really started something. What did Bo have to say?"

"At first he balked at taking 'charity' but Carina and I pointed out that they had a legit problem. There was no reason that his family had to suffer privation when it wasn't necessary. There are all sorts of programs set up to handle these contingencies."

"So he agreed?" said Zain in a rather incredulous voice.

"He didn't object. He just went back to treating a sick cow."

Not one to remain silent for long, Hawk said, "Don't get sore, but I didn't include any shots of your house. That wouldn't help the image we're trying to build. They can't very well be victims, whiles living in a house like that."

Rose didn't like the direction the conversation was going, so she injected, "The water is down about midway on the ground floor. When we flew out, we followed the river down. There is a constriction in the channel that is slowing the runoff. The areas that have been exposed are covered with muck....and it stinks.

Hawk stood. "I've got to get some sleep. I'm going out with Guard helicopter in the morning. We load at ten. Are you coming my dear?"

Rose frowned momentarily at Hawk's familiarity before smiling sweetly and replying, "No, I have to help Zain get the trailer loaded. I know you can handle it. Keep up the good work. Maybe there will be a Pulitzer prize in there somewhere."

Hawk smoothed his hair and strutted out of the restaurant.

"Oh, he's a pain in the ass, but pliable enough to be useful," said Rose when the reporter was out of earshot.

Zain wondered if Rose thought he was pliable like Hunter

"What's on the agenda for this afternoon?" said Rose. "Oh, yes. I have the $500 gift certificate from the Food Pantry. It just dawned on me that we can't take anything that needs refrigeration. It'll spoil before we can get it back. That even reduces the fresh vegetables we can take back."

"There are some things that will last and I've picked up several coolers we can ice down. "And," said Zain with a self-satisfied smile, "I found some dry ice. We can even take some ice cream back as a treat for the kids."

Rose reached across the table to pat his hand. "Always thinking, aren't you?"

"Doesn't everyone?" said Zain rather lamely.

Zain's schedule put them back on the tractor on the third day. They had the remainder of that day and one more to complete their buying, loading and returning of the truck.

The next morning, under the threat of having to get his son up and fed while his wife, Pamela, picked up Zain and Rose at the Continental, District Court Judge Raymond Livingston Winters volunteered to run the taxi service. When the judge pulled his Lexus back into his driveway with Zain and Rose, he found a sizeable contingent waiting. Hunter Hawk was there complete with a cameraman and a relay truck for a live feed for the early morning news.

"What's all this?" asked Zain.

"It's probably a product of Hawk's mind. He'll milk this for all it's worth. There's probably some county dignitaries out here to get some face time," said Rose with a chuckle. Zain could see she was enjoying the fruits of the seeds she'd sown.

After all the glad-handing and well-wishing from the business and civic leaders that Hawk had lined up, Zain set the magneto and turned the flywheel. On the first turn there was a great belch of smoke from the stack and the tractor shuddered into life. Zain adjusted the spark and gave Rose a hand-up. She settled into her seat. After a bright smile and an energetic wave, Zain shifted into gear. Slowly the tractor and its heavily loaded trailer moved forward, gaining speed to its 2.5MPH top range.

At noon, the Channel six helicopter crew found them passing through rough, tree studded country. Hawk waved and Zain and Rose waved back.

The trip back took longer than the trip out. Zain had to take extra care not to flip the top-heavy trailer. After the helicopter left, Zain pulled into the shade of a tree and stopped. "Let's take a break."

"Don't say that word. I think mine is....Rose slowly swung her leg over the seat to dismount.

"The sandwiches Pamela Winters sent along are in the top of the first ice chest. Will you get them while I put some kerosene in the tractor?"

Rose pulled out a lunch hamper and settled down far enough away to get a little relief from the incessant tractor noise.

Zain stretched to get some of the kinks out before plopping down beside Rose.

Chicken or salami and cheese?"

"Salami, please."

"What's on the agenda when we get back?"

"As soon as the water goes down enough, I've got to start rebuilding the road so I don't have to make this trip again. But, while waiting for things to dry out, I'll cut new poles for the electrical lines. I'll be able to salvage some, but a bunch will be lost. I'll try to reuse as much wire as possible. That stuff gets expensive."

"How will you fix the road?"

"This old tractor has a blade. With the exception of the Vasa ranch, the rest of the road is on my land. I'll just take the line of least resistance. I'd like to salvage as much of the graveled surface as possible."

"How come the Vasa place sits right in the middle of your land?"

"Bo's original house was here when the Graffs bought the property. It became the ranch foreman's residence after the big house was built. As I get the story, the sisters got hard up for money. They sold the house with enough land to make a decent small ranch. It went through several owners before Bo and Carina bought it."

After lunch, Zain again headed the tractor west and the trip resumed except for fuel stops. Zain kept the wheels rotating so they would arrive before the light gave out.

The kids heard the tractor long before it crested the last hill. Erik and Emil raced across the pasture to open the gate. They weren't content to wait for the tractor to get there. They continued on up the hill as fast as they could over broken ground.

Zain eased up on the speed. He didn't want to grind the kids under the great, steel wheels as the pair leaped aboard the tractor, squeezing in between the driver and the fenders. They were patting both Zain and Rose on the arms and shoulders and talking up a storm, all of which was drowned out by the engine.

The rest of the family waited at the edge of the yard. The kids were excited. All the barn yard animals fled before the tractor racket and the wild antics of the kids.

Zain pointed at the stable and continue on into the cave that ran down the middle. He didn't want to stop outside and then have to get back on the beast later to move it under shelter.

When the tractor finally went silent, both Zain and Rose sat for a moment before stiffly dismounting. There was little light in the stable but the Vasas found the weary pair. Carina hugged Rose. Bo extended a callused hand, saying, "Welcome home."

The kids were swarming over the tractor. Zain yelled over the hubbub, " Erik, Emil, get those four blue ice chests into the kitchen.

"Bo, see that big crate on the back end. We need to unload it tonight. It's a generator that is big enough to run the refrigerator and freezer. There is also a cardboard box with wire and connectors near there."

"The generator can wait until after dinner," declared Carina. "You guys need to eat and rest. Go get cleaned up and be ready to eat in twenty minutes. Don't be late. It's been hard keeping this pack of hungry Vikings from gnawing their way through the kitchen door. Shoo, shoo."

Zain and Rose trudged off to the house while the rest unloaded the ice chests. A good hot shower did both of them a world of good. They even made Carina's time schedule. She was carrying a huge tureen of beef stew through the kitchen door as the travelers came in from the hall.

Carina served the kids first because they were ravenous due to the late hour and they were vying to tell their latest story or ask Rose the most important question in the whole world. After a couple of stern warnings about talking with their mouths full, the adults were able to converse.

"I'm so glad to get that generator so we can have refrigeration and freezing," said Carina. "This is the last of the meat that came in on the helicopter. One more day and it probably would have spoiled. We'll lose some produce and fruit if we don't get it in the refrigerator. Whoever selected the groceries apparently didn't think about us not having electricity. I hate to waste anything. Don't get me wrong, we're really glad to get the food."

Bo concentrated on his plate.

"There's a couple of chests with dry ice," said Zain. "They should hold until the stuff can be transferred. However, there is one thing that should be taken out now."

Zain excused himself from the table and disappeared

into the kitchen. A couple of minutes later he reappeared carrying a gallon of ice cream.

A cheer went up from the kids.

"One of the worse things about not having electricity," said Zain, "is not to have anything cold to drink. I'm tired of drinking warm beer."

Inga wrinkled her nose. "Warm colas are yukkie too."

With hunger partially appeased, conversation became the next item on the agenda. All eight wanted to talk at once. To regain some semblance of order, Bo slapped the table with his big, hard hand. He pointed at Elen. "You first....then Elsa and on around the table."

Little Elen got so excited she forgot what she wanted to say. Bo pointed at Elsa.

"Did you see any deer when you went to town?"

Rose fielded that question. "No. That tractor makes so much racket it scared them away."

The questions and the stories ran on through the meal and during the prolonged period as they waited for the ice cream to get soft enough to serve.

After dessert, Zain and Bo headed out to hook up the generator. The older boys trailed along, leaving the rest to clear the table and deal with the dishes.

It was late before the generator was installed, fueled and hooked up. Zain needed another shower. Rose was already in bed reading. She put her book away as he slid onto his edge of the bed.

After some small talk, Rose seemed to marshal her courage. "You know there is another helicopter trip scheduled for tomorrow?"

"Yeah. Is Hunter coming along"

"I don't know."

Zain didn't say anything.

"I'm going to hitch a ride back to town. I have delayed longer than I had planned."

"Oh," said Zain and immediately he felt foolish for inflecting it to sound as if he would feel sorry about her leaving. He would feel sorry she was leaving, but he hadn't intended to convey that feeling.

Rose was quick to explain. "I have a time schedule I must meet. It's very important to me."

"What I meant was, with all that's going on, I'd completely forgotten you'd said you were on a schedule. I'm sorry I couldn't get those modeling photos printed. I think they're going to be great."

"While we were in town, I called my friend Blade. He's the top cutter in the Seattle area. At one time he was one of the best tattoo artists in the country, but he gave it up for other things. Let me show you something." Rose slid off the bed to get her knapsack.

Zain mentally rolled his eyes. Rose had an appointment with a hairdresser.

Rose carefully extracted a plywood box that was approximately 10x10x2. The top was tied on with a string. She removed the top and pulled out a sealed plastic bag. Zain could see it contained a small set of cake watercolors and an assortment of brushes. Beneath was a brown paper wrapped package. Rose slowly unfolded the flaps to reveal a watercolor painting of wild roses on what looked like 400 lb. paper.

She placed the small painting on the bed so Zain could see it. "This is the final study for here." She slapped the bare spot on her right hip.

Zain turned to sit cross-legged on the bed so he could bend forward for a closer look at the little painting.

"It's beautiful," said Zain with the passion he reserved for exceptionally creative efforts. "Is this yours?"

Rose straightened up to look him straight in the eye. "Whose did you think it would be?"

"You never said you were a painter," said Zain

defensively.

"I'm not a painter. I just paint wild roses."

"Well, you paint wild roses beautifully."

"It's kind of a memorial to my mother. She did them so well, and after she died I didn't have a single example left. She'd sold everything to keep me in school. I used her studies as patterns and then I tried to remember her style. I'm afraid I ultimately developed my own style instead of perpetuating her's."

Rose was blinking away tears.

Zain quelled the impulse to take her in his arms to offer comfort. That would appear that he was taking advantage of the situation. He contented himself with, "Any serious artist would be pleased, indeed, if her offspring could develop a style of her own. That's what all artists attempt. Few really succeed."

"As a favor, Blade started this tattoo two years ago. He faithfully reproduced my paintings and seamlessly integrated them with the last ones. He's a master, but he's dying and he wants to finish this before it's too late. I have to leave."

Rose carefully rewrapped her little paintings, leaving Zain wondering what to say. He could see the emotion playing all over her face. She was dealing with situations that were important to her. On one hand, he couldn't understand the value she was placing on a tattoo, but on the other hand he didn't want to trivialize her feelings. He ended up lamely saying, "In the morning, I'll write you a check for the modeling sessions. I'll include the fee you missed from my drawing class."

A silence hung in the air as Rose returned her back pack to its place against the wall. She returned to her side of the bed and pulled the sheet up to her chin. "The school fee isn't your responsibility. Forget it. If my schedule permits, I'll stop by the school to model for Devon. The model yawned broadly, said, “Good night” and snuggled down into her pillow.

“This is a really lousy ending to a day,” thought Zain as he blew out the lamp and settled down. He was finding himself strongly attracted to the girl next to him. She ranked very high on his mental checklist of prerequisites. Her physical attributes fell either in the categories of desirable or acceptable. He really liked her personality and mental proclivities.

On the negative side, he didn’t hold anyone who would mutilate her body with tattoos in very high esteem.... especially with someone who carried it to Rose’s extreme.

Then there was the attitude that those who had, should provide for those who hadn’t. She didn’t realize how her helicopter flight with all the freebees had affected Bo. He’d dedicated his life to his family, and that flight said to the whole world that he couldn’t care for his family. At least in his own mind, his value had been greatly diminished. That tractor trip had been a cooperative effort. Bo had contributed his brawn to getting the expedition ready and agreed to watch the home front despite his own desire to accompany Zain. He’d also thrown his limited financial help plus a substantial credit rating into the effort. His family wouldn’t have suffered any privation before the tractor had returned, but the with the TV coverage the whole world knew he had failed as a provider.

From their conversations, Zain had come to the conclusion that Rose was well versed in how to play the freebee game. She could always get free meals, clothes, medical care or whatever she needed by accessing the host of government agencies, religious organizations, or civic groups that dealt in that realm.

Zain wasn’t the only one feigning sleep. Rose was wondering what had gone wrong. There was a acre of bed sheet between her and a naked man. Here she was leaving the next day. It was his last chance to make a play for her....and he was sleeping. She wondered if something was wrong with her. Of course, maybe he was gay. That would have been the easy answer, but for some reason she didn't think that that was it. It was probably something like he was so straight he was saving himself for a virgin bride. That thought didn't quite hit the mark either. It looked as if she was just going to have to fantasize.

Chapter 8

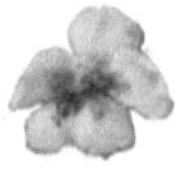

Zain was horribly stiff in the morning, both from the bouncy tractor ride and perching on the edge of the bed as he tried not to move so as to not disturb his roommate. Rose had already vacated the bedroom. From the hubbub coming from the bathroom, he could tell she was joshing with the kids. Zain made his way to the desk where he wrote out a check for the modeling fees. He had second thoughts. A check might be hard for her to handle, so he tapped his cash reserve.

He put the five twenties on Rose's backpack before he joined the bathroom throng. He and Rose passed in the doorway with a mutual "good morning." Zain was still in the shower when the breakfast bell sounded. That quickly cleared the bathroom.

Breakfast conversation centered around the helicopter arrival and Rose's imminent departure. As soon as breakfast was over, Bo and Zain, along with Erik and Emil, headed for the stables to unload the trailer. They wanted to use it to off-load the goods coming in on the helicopter.

"What's all the pvc for?" asked Bo as he circled the trailer looking for a place to start.

"There's enough pipe to run a line from my cistern to your house. Buried down in the stack of stuff is a gas-operated pressure cleaner. You can use it to flush the mud out of your house. I'm going to need one this spring before I paint. I wonder how long it's been since this place saw a paint brush? I thought we could share the expense."

"You've got a deal. While you were gone, I waded into the house. There is at least six inches of mud in there. I'll have to shovel or scrape most of it out. I was wondering how I'd get it clean."

"Later, after the water gets away from your well, you can use the spring water to help flush out the contaminated stuff. How about having the boys wrestle those ice chests to the house? Carina needs to do something with the perishables."

Zain and Bo started shifting the sacks of grain so the kids could feed the animals.

As soon as they could manage it, the rest of the kids escaped from the kitchen ostensibly to feed the critters. Inga had her Pot Bellied pig tracking along at her heels. The rest of the youngsters each had their own entourage in tow.

All the kids were scanning the horizon for the military helicopter. Elsa, the youngest of the bunch was the one to spot the speck in the distance, much to the consternation of the rest.

Carina and Rose came out to keep the kids out of the copter rotors and greet the crew. Rose was in her traveling jeans, and her pony tail was pulled through the little Mexican sombrero. Her backpack was sitting off to the side.

As soon as the pilot cut the power, there was a sixteen foot stampede toward the side door. The first out was Hunter Hawk, followed by his photographer, who was getting shots of the excited kids clamoring around the TV personality.

Then Hunter broke away to warmly greet Carina and, especially, Rose.

The cameraman swung around to follow the progress of the loud, antique tractor. Bo was driving and Zain was dangling his feet off the side of the trailer. Bo executed a wide turn so he could bring the trailer to the unloading door. As soon as it was in place, the military crew started unloading. The first item was a gigantic gray bundle confined with steel bands. It took all hands to roll it out of the aircraft and onto the trailer.

"What is that?" said Carina as she stepped forward to peer at the bundle of fabric.

Hawk laughed. "That is a donation from Grasshopper Silk Screen plant. They screened a whole order of PE shorts and T-shirts for Canyon Junior High School. Someone forgot the 'Junior'. When the boss heard about all your kids, he sent this bundle along instead of selling it to the open market trade in Mexico. They're all sizes. Don't cut the bundle until you have it where you want it. That thing will virtually explode. I wish I could hang around to see that."

As the transfer of food stuffs and critter fodder proceeded, Rose climbed up to talk to the pilot. A few minutes later, she retrieved her backpack and passed it up to the pilot. Then she moved over to Carina. The two women hugged. The three younger sets of twins gathered around to get their hugs. Erik and Emil stayed with the men, having passed beyond the hug-stage in their lives. The photographer was taking it all in.

When Hawk tried to horn in on the good-byes to pad his story, Rose dismissed him by, "I'm going out on the chopper. I can talk to you later."

The last sacks of feed were hoisted onto the top of the stack on the trailer. Erik and Emil were on top of the feed. Rose reached up to shake hands with both. She also shook Bo's hand. Zain jumped down from the trailer with a proffered hand. Rose grasped it firmly and then pulled him forward and down so she could kiss him on the cheek. "Thanks, you big lug. Keep sculpting. I want to see your name in lights."

The kiss caught Zain completely by surprise. By the time he regrouped, Rose had vaulted up on the trailer and stepped into the helicopter.

Bo revved up the tractor engine and pulled away. The helicopter blades started to turn, forcing everyone to retreat. Hawk and the cameraman jumped aboard.

As the lithe, jean-clad female became smaller and smaller, Zain experienced an oppressive sense of loss. He'd been having little twinges since Rose had announced her impending departure, but the power of his current feelings surprised and concerned him. The pair continued to wave until the copter turned and headed down river.

When Zain turned his attention back to the here and now, he found the whole Vasa family smiling at him.

"I think she likes you," declared Inga.

"Yeah, she kissed him," said Elen, who was still young enough to always state the obvious with great authority.

"Yuk," said Kas.

Zain felt a blush coming on so he jumped up on the trailer and waved Bo toward the stables.

Kas ran alongside shouting, "I want to see the bundle explode."

Zain jumped down to open one of the vacant stall doors. He motioned for Bo to pull up along the door so they could roll the clothing bundle directly into the stall.

Armed with metal sheers from the studio, Zain eyed the two steel binding bands. They were holding some heavy compaction. Deciding to heed Hunter's warning, he waived the kids out the door. He chuckled at the precision drill. The little ones were on their bellies on the floor. The next oldest went to hands and knees on each side of the door, peering around the jamb. Inga and Inger stooped over so the two first-borns could see over the top. Bo and Carina stood behind. Zain had noted this size-grading in any number of situations.

Zain leaned over the bundle to snip the far-side band. "Zing," went the cut metal ribbon as is whipped out. There was a loud whoof as the air became filled with gray cotton. The whole bundle collapsed.

"Wow," yelled Kas as he led the charge into the stable and executed a grand belly flop in the center of the heap.

Carina moved in to inspect the clothes. There were hundreds of large, medium and small elastic banded shorts and T-shirts. The shorts were emblazoned with "Canyon High School on the left leg. The lettering was on the left breast of the shirts.

"There's enough here to keep this horde of Vikings in play clothes until we have an empty nest. Zain, will you take a picture of them to send to the donor?"

"Sure, any time you want. Right now we'd better get the trailer unloaded."

Although he didn't grouse, Bo still wasn't happy with the donations. Occasionally, he posed a pointed question such as, "What are we supposed to do with a full crate of celery?"

Inga countered, "Oh, Matilda loves celery."

"We've got enough food to keep her going until she dies of old age," grumbled Bo.

Zain laughed. "Matilda earned every pound of that food with the hungry act she was putting on when Hunter was filming her. She and Inga stole the show. After we can get out, I'll try to get a copy of the program."

Chapter 9

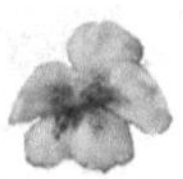

The next morning, the water dropped below the floor level. Bo and Carina waded through the remaining water to inspect their home. Zain stayed with the kids on dry land. Fortunately, Bo had left the doors open. It would have taken weeks for the closed, water-swelled doors to dry enough to open.

Both adults looked somber as they waded back, but Carina brightened as she got to the kids. “Everything is still there. It’s just dirty. As soon as we get it cleaned up and dried out, we can move back home. After lunch, we’ll get started.”

As Zain and Bo headed back to the stable, Zain said, “How is it?”

“That’s a good old farmhouse. Sturdy. All the floor coverings are shot. So is all the flimsy paneling on the walls, but the original diagonal shiplap walls are still there. There’s a lot of warping, but I can take care of that. All the doors, except one, are solid wood. There’s one of those hollow core doors on the new closet—that disintegrated.”

“It looks as if you lost some windows.”

"Yeah, a few are gone on the first floor. That's no problem. The frames are still good. I'll just need some glass, points and putty. It'll be a long time before they dry out enough to open. Do you have any garden tools....shovels, hoes.... anything to move muck?"

"The old carriage house has some. You're welcome to whatever you need. I think I'll start running that pvc line."

"I can do that. You have other things to do."

"It won't take long to glue those things together. You get the kids working on the house. After I finish with the pvc, I'm going to that stand of lodge-pole pines to cut poles for the electrical line. Later, I'll need your help loading them onto the trailer."

"I figure it's just as much to my advantage as yours to get that road open and the electrical and phone working. I'm going to let the family do most of the cleaning. By the time the poles are ready, I can cut Erik and Emil loose from cleaning to add some more muscle."

Zain smiled at Bo's smile. The boys would be a little light to do much of the heavy hauling, but Bo would be teaching them how to work. Zain had never thought much about being a father, but if he ever became one, he had a good model in Bo Vasa.

"By the time I get new poles cut, we should be able to take the tractor down the valley. There'll be a bunch of washouts. I have a blade for the tractor. There is also a power auger....if I can figure out how to use it."

"I know a little about these things. We can figure it out."

"One of the important items is to salvage as much wire as possible. That stuff is expensive when you're talking about three miles."

Zain had laid out the pvc lengths from his cistern to Bo's yard and Bo had collected all the available tools to begin the house cleanup by the time Carina called them to lunch.

The kids had already changed into their gym clothes to keep from mucking up their regular clothes. It appeared that the standard uniform was to be shorts on the boys and shirts on the girls. The shirts were selected so as to be short shifts. Carina got into the act, but she wore both tops and bottoms.

After lunch the dishes were stacked in the sink awaiting later attention. Bo led his work party down the hill to start the clean-up. Zain grabbed a bag of couplings and a can of pvc glue and set out to hookup the pipe. From his vantage point uphill, he chuckled to see Carina, always the pragmatist, have the kids strip off their new gym clothes before sloshing to the house. She wasn't about to let them generate a bigger pile of laundry than she already had.

As the afternoon progressed, tons of mud were shoved out the back door and pitched out broken windows. As Zain worked his way toward the house, he could hear round singing in Swedish. Carina sang the question and Bo led the chorus of lust voices in the reply. Zain ran out of pipe just as he hit the high water mark. Hoses would have to bridge the remaining gap.

Zain glued on the terminal coupling and screwed in the hose bib before he trudged back up the hill to the cistern to turn on the water so he could check for leaks.

The next morning, Zain loaded the chain saw, gas can, and chain saw oil on the trailer before driving the bellowing heap of iron up the hill toward the stand of lodge pole pine. He had to make a couple of detours to get through gates. As he approached the patch, he could see that there were many blow-downs from the high winds generated by the storm.

Starting with the blow-downs, Zain trimmed the sound ones to 20 foot lengths. The broken ones that were in his way were bucked up into firewood. Outside of requiring the necessary safety precautions, it was a brainless job, which freed mental time for Zain to plan his new sculpture series. He was getting anxious to begin. He'd been out of the studio much too long.

Zain also found Rose tracking back and forth through his thoughts. She was an enigma. On one hand she lives like a vagabond. She assumes no responsibilities and then she has that bloody tattoo. Tattoos had always been his symbol of the counter-cultures that represented the tenants that he didn't much value.

On the other hand, he couldn't get her out of his mind. For the umpteenth time he wondered if he should have made a pass at her. They'd slept naked in the same bed for many nights. But, he had a steadfast policy of not trying to put his pecker into hired help. Besides, she'd put him on notice that her weekend stay was not an invitation into her bed. Of course, it was circumstances that had put them in the same bed, but he didn't feel free to take advantage of the situation.

Zain shook his head to get his thoughts back to the series. The sun had passed its zenith and it was dropping fast toward the mountains. He should have taken up Carina's offer of a lunch. He contented himself with a swig of warm water. Since he didn't know how many poles he would need, he decided not to cut any more until there was a count.

As he chugged down the hill toward the house, he had to laugh at the sight that presented itself. Bo was standing with the pvc pipe on his shoulder providing an improvised shower. Carina was supervising the demudding of her eight naked kids.

Erik and Emil got a special dispensation to escape the family group to help Zain. As they fueled the tractor, cleaned, and stowed the tools, Zain asked, "How'd the cleaning go?"

"When you try to push a pile of stuff, your feet slide out

from under you. It's hard work," said Emil.

"Dad said we'll start using the pressure washer tomorrow. When that stuff dries out it's like concrete," said Erik. "I hope that washing takes the smell away."

After dinner, Zain announced that the next day he was planning on taking the tractor down the valley as far as possible to survey the damage to the road, count how many power poles he'd need, and salvage any wire he could find. Bo offered to go along, but Zain declined the offer, saying that he wasn't planning to do anything but observe.

"One thing that doesn't seem right, is that the water should be receding faster," said Zain. Rose told me that she'd seen a backup down at the narrows. If I can get that far, I'll check it out."

The next morning, Zain accepted the sack lunch Carina wanted to prepare for him. By the time he'd replaced his improvised rumble seat with a cargo box for a jerry can, tools and lunch, the Vasas were already swarming over their house. Great piles of mud were in evidence at every window and the door. As he spun the flywheel to start the tractor, he heard Bo fire up the pressure washer.

Before starting his trek downstream, he delayed long enough to clear his driveway of five downed poplars. On the way back, he'd drag one up for firewood.

Over the years, surface material had been added to the roadway so that it was elevated enough over the general terrain for Zain to follow it on the tractor. Mud was everywhere. There were still ponds of standing water.

The washout that Zain had been able to see from the house was a major one, but it looked as if there was enough solid land to the uphill side that vehicles could circumvent it in fair weather or during the winter freeze. During wet weather, vehicles might get bogged down. Two power poles were missing there.

As Zain moved down the valley, he found several gullies

through the road caused by runoff from the uplands. Most could be easily filled. The water coming down the valley had eaten into the road in many places. Instead of trying to fill the washouts, he'd just move the road bed to solid ground.

When he got down to the narrows that had caused the water to backup, disaster leered at him. The entire area had been scoured away down to bed rock. Zain pulled to the edge of the high ground and walked up to the crest. Any trace of his road all the way to where it had joined the county road, had vanished.

Zain had a big lump in his stomach. To this point, everything had been manageable. He and Bo could deal with the road. It was not as if they had to observe legal right-of-ways. They owned all the land. There were twenty-seven poles that needed replacement or repositioning, which they could handle too. All his fences were gone, but that didn't matter since he didn't run any livestock. Bo would have to replace his fences before he could run his stock on the flooded pastures.

However, the narrows were another thing. Hundreds of cubic yards of earth were gone. All that was left was the bare rock of the promontories and the base level rock. The walls of the narrows were too steep for vehicles to traverse or go over.

Beyond the narrows was a gigantic dam of debris stacked against the county bridge, creating a lake. The county crews that were working on the dam looked like ants as they crawled through the tree and root systems. The broken lumber was probably from Bo's out-buildings. Zain couldn't take the tractor to the bridge through the narrows. He'd have to retreat upstream until he found a gentler slope. Getting off the high ground on the other side might be a problem. It would be easier to walk over.

However, before heading over to the bridge, Zain would

eat the lunch Carina had sent along. He returned to the idling tractor for his sandwich. As he was returning to his vantage point overlooking the dam, a powerful explosion threw a great plume of debris skyward. Chunks of wood and rock rained down on where he had been sitting a few minutes earlier. Nothing hit close to him, but he waited until the debris shower was over before resuming his seat on his rock. It was fortunate that he had decided to eat lunch first.

The smoke and the water vapor cleared. The work crews were standing around their vehicles, which they had moved some distance down the road toward town. From their movements, it appeared they had just become aware of Zain's proximity to the blast area.

The work crews returned to their work. Zain finished his sandwich, stuffed the empty sack into his pocket and started hiking around the dam, which was now draining.

A pot-bellied man in a yellow hard hat came out to meet Zain as he walked down the road to the work area.

"Man, I'm sorry. I didn't know anyone was there."

"No harm. I was out of the way when the blast went off."

"That's a relief. I'm Jake Coleman, the foreman on this job."

"Zain Zook. I live up the river. I'm surveying the damage to my road and electrical lines."

"How is it on the other side of the narrows?"

"There are some washouts. With a little filling and a detour here and there, we'll be able to get here. But, that's not going to do me much good is it? What are you planning to do?"

"First, we have get rid of all this debris. It looks as if we were successful in opening a channel to drain the lake. Then we are to build up the road bed. It's been heavily eroded. Then to keep the road, we're going to have to get the river back in its channel. If we don't, then every time there's a heavy rain, the water will take out the bridge approaches."

"There was also a ramp for me to get up to the road level."

"We're still working on the best way to get this fixed. Is there just you back there?"

"No, there's another family with eight kids that will have to be getting to school pretty soon."

"Oh, you're the ones that had the helicopter relief flights."

"Yeah. We're still cut off. Before long I'll have to make another supply run over the hills in the tractor unless we can get through here.

"I wouldn't count on anything soon, but what do I know? I'm only the foreman on a road crew. I do know that there is a lot of high-level discussions going on. Something is going to have to be done about those three dams. They're needed for flood control."

"They certainly didn't help much this time," said Zain with more than a little derision in his voice.

The foreman came back defensively. "This was the storm of the century. In between those century storms, those little dams have done their job. The problem now is that those dams are on Federal Bureau of Land Management lands. They were built and serviced from a shelf road on the upper side. That road, in large part, no longer exists. Great mud slides wiped out large sections. The cost of replacing that road is prohibitive. I think they are looking at going up the valley."

"Hmm," said Zain. "Since Bo and I own all that land from the narrows up to BLM, I think we should expect visitors."

The foreman smiled. "I suspect so. Don't let them off the hook easy-like. If they can't go up the valley, they're hurting."

The foreman turned to inspect the diminishing lake. "I've

got to get back. We have to place another charge. That should drain the lake. We're going to burn a lot of that stuff in place if the weather cooperates. Good Luck."

As Zain hiked back to the tractor, he speculated on what he would ask in return for an easement across his property. There were many things to consider, such as, route, road surface, maintenance, fencing, crossing for livestock and such things. Also he didn't want that road to open his lands to the public. Presently, he was pretty much isolated from hunting, fishing, and ATVs.

That night at dinner, the conversation was pretty much adult talk concerning road easements and such. The kids excused themselves as early as possible to adjourn to the game room.

By the time the after dinner coffee was consumed, Zain and the Vasas had decided on a plan of action if the county came asking. Erik poked his head into the dining room to see what was happening. His mother took the opportunity to send him to collect the other twins for KP duty.

Zain had noticed that Erik and, to a lesser extent, Emil were frequently checking on his activities. It appeared they didn't want to be left out of anything interesting that Zain might be doing. Zain found a considerable amount of his time was used to explain something to the boys.

The preceding day, Zain had checked the humidity of the clay in the clay safe. It had to be kept at a constant water consistency so that it was not too rigid nor too soupy. By the time the two boys ran out of questions, they had received a full college course in the care of clay.

This evening was not to be an exception. As soon as Zain moved the kitchen table to a space next to the refrigerator, both the 13 year-olds were wanting to know what was going on.

"I'm going to use the generator to power the printer so I can print some pictures of Rose. My printer can read directly from my memory card. It's not as good as being able to work with the photos on my computer, but it's better than waiting until we get electricity. If you can get away from your mother, you can help me carry some stuff downstairs."

"Mom," yelled the twins in unison.

Carina gave Zain a baleful, defeated look as she gave a dismissive gesture to her first-borns.

Zain led his team upstairs. Ten minutes later they returned. Zain carried his printer. The boys had the various papers, extra ink cartridges, memory chips, and implements that Zain had laid out.

"The questions were already starting. "Why do you have two different papers?" asked Emil.

"The glossy photo paper is expensive. I can get the same information off a plain paper print at a fraction of the cost. The same is true with the colored ink. The best view of the pose will be printed in color on photo paper. I'll use black ink on plain paper for the rest. I wish I had a cropping capacity with this machine. That would save a lot of ink and time."

The first images in the print queue were front, back, and side shots of Rose standing straight up with her feet slightly apart and her hands hanging to her sides. They were printed on good paper.

"What are those for?" said Erik. "They're kinda boring."

Zain had to smile. A few days ago he'd never have expected to hear such a comment from a thirteen-year-old-boy while looking at pictures of a good-looking naked lady. "I'll use those to make the armature....the frame that is on the inside of the figure to hold up the clay."

When the back view had been printed, Zain, using a ball point pen and a ruler, drew a stick figure on the print.

A line went from the top of the head down the spine to the hips. Horizontal lines connected the two shoulder joints and the two hip points. Lines were drawn along the arms and legs. The elbows and the knee positions were noted.

"Whatcha doing?" said Emil, as Zain started measuring the various lines with a meter scale.

"It's easier to use the decimal system than fractions."

"Why?"

"Well, let's say we want to sculpt this figure five times larger than this image on the photograph. That means each of these lines has to be measured and then multiplied by five. This line is 1 and 17/32s inches." He remeasured the mark with the metric scale. "In the metric system it is 4 centimeters. Which is easier to multiple?"

"Jeeze," said Erik. "You have to use math even in sculpture?"

"You bet. You'd better learn it well. You won't get far without math." Zain suppressed a smile as he glanced over Erik's shoulder to catch Carina giving him a thumbs up.

The printer was still working its way through the print queue when the kids were chased off to bed.

Bo and Carina took over the boys' chairs. They were obviously concerned. Zain figured Bo wanted to ask for something, but he was having a hard time popping the question. He normally pulled his own freight. To do otherwise went against his basic personality.

Zain started out the conversation. "How's the house coming?"

"We've got the mud out. Tomorrow I'll start tearing out the paneling. I'll leave everything open until the shiplap dries out. I can nail down any warpage. It'll be a while before I'll be about to get paneling up again."

"I saw you flushing mud out of the barn. Any damage there?"

"It's just a nasty cleaning job. The water didn't get into the hay. I got all the loose equipment into the mow before the water got there."

"When do you think we can get electricity?" said Carina. "We could move back into the house as soon as it dries out a little more, but we have an electric stove."

"Don't worry about moving yet. You're not bothering me. Besides, as soon as you leave I'll have to start eating my own cooking again."

"I don't think that would be much of hardship on you. You seem to know your way around a kitchen."

"That may be true, but I hate doing dishes."

Bo emphatically nodded his head in agreement.

Bo still hadn't brought up the topic that was worrying him. Zain thought he knew what was bothering his neighbor. Now that the water was gone, all of Bo's grazing land and hay land were covered with a thick layer of mud. It wouldn't be until spring before any grass could work its way through. Once it did poke its way through, it would probably be lush with all the new nutrients that had washed in.

But, in the meantime, Bo was out of business unless he could leave his livestock on Zain's property. He couldn't afford to feed them hay until spring.

"I've been thinking," said Zain. "There hasn't been any stock on this place for fifty or so years. I've never gone over the entire property. It must be pretty well overgrown by now. It won't hold as many cattle as it once would have, but there should be plenty of grazing for your herd until the snow flies and you have to start feeding. It would help me considerably if you'd leave your livestock on the uplands for a while.

"There's another thousand acres up the canyon that backs up against BLM land. It's supposed to be fenced, but someone would have to ride the fences to patch any breaks.

"On down the line, after all this flood mess is history, maybe we can work out some sort of agreement should you want to expand your herd."

Carina was having difficulty suppressing a smile. Bo was clearing his throat while keeping a serious demeanor. He was minutely examining the stove pipe where it entered the flue.

In a contemplative, measured tone Bo said, “Well, I think something can be arranged.”

With a burst of joyous laughter, Carina lost her battle. Her chair careened across the room as she jumped up to hug her husband. A broad, smiling face appeared from behind Carina’s shoulder. Bo disengaged his right hand and stuck it out to Zain. “Thanks, neighbor. You don’t know what this means. I’d have had to sell my stock, and this is the wrong time of the year. It would have meant giving up the ranch and going to work for someone else. That would be a hard thing for me to do.”

“I don’t suppose,” said Zain, “that it’s going to be easy staying here, but I bet you can get through it.”

CHAPTER 10

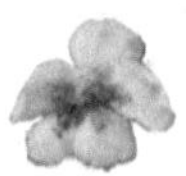

The next day, Zain was going through the Vasa house with Bo, making a list of supplies that would be needed to get the place habitable again. The structure was drying out under the hot, summer winds. The two men were interrupted by Carina warning the kids to get covered up. A vehicle was coming up the valley.

What had once been a white, four-wheel drive utility vehicle slowly picked its way along the carcass of the old road. A county emblem on the door was still distinguishable.

"They're probably coming to see you," said Bo.

"Whatever it is, it involves both of us."

The two occupants of the vehicle waved at the kids, but the vehicle continued on toward the big house.

"We'd better go see what they want," said Zain as he led the way across the Vasa yard and up the hill. Zain waved the driver around the house to the back door.

"Hi, I'm Dade Scott and this is Phil Martini. We're from the county commissioner's office. We need to talk to you about a whole laundry list of things."

Zain suggested that they adjourn to the dining room when he saw the armload of maps Martini was dragging out of the back seat. The meeting turned into a marathon negotiating session. Carina kept the coffee cups full and the kids out of sight and sound. She fed the kids at noon and then brought sandwiches in for the men.

The sun was getting low in the sky before the county men headed down the valley.

At dinner, Zain told Carina and the kids the salient part of the negotiations. "The reason the county men were here is that it has been established that the three dams have to be rebuilt because they are a vital part of the state flood control program. The problem is that when the dams were built, the construction crews came in from the south along an old shelf-road. However, the storm took out large sections of the road. It would be prohibitive to blast a whole new shelf. That is why they are being so considerate of our needs. It is far cheaper to come in from this end.

"This is a federal, state and county joint effort. Because they need right-of-ways from us, they will build a two-way road up to my drive. Then they will punch an access road on up to the dam site. There will be a gate so the public can be kept out. Our road will be fenced and stock crossings will be provided."

"What about electricity?" said Carina.

"There is a transmission line on BLM land along my back property line. They will arrange for a drop for us. That will mean about a third as much wire as going down the valley to the county road. I hope we can salvage enough copper to make the run."

"What about the telephone?" said Inga. "I haven't talked to my friends all summer."

Bo fielded that question. "If the telephone line over the mountain is out, they may bring one from this side and we can tie into it."

"They were thinking they could use cell phones, but the last time I tried to use a cell," said Zain, "there wasn't a strong enough signal. It may be a while before we have phone service."

"Ugh," came a chorus from the older twins.

The next morning, Zain was up as early as Bo. Instead of milking cows, Zain headed for his studio. The first item of business was to weld up a couple of armatures for the two-foot figures. Then the armatures were bolted to wooden work bases. Next he mounted two sets of Rose photographs to large plywood panels.

When Carina called Zain to breakfast, Erik and Emil realized Zain had sneaked out on them and had been working in the studio. They were really put out at their mother for not calling them. There was no telling what they had missed.

This led to a pleading match. The twins were trying to trade off their work schedule in their house for helping Zain in the studio. They won only a ten-minute reprieve before they had to report to work in the house.

The driving fascination of the moment for the boys became oxygen/acetylene welding and iron working. They were heartened to learn that Zain would be needing many more armatures and that if they learned to weld, they could take over that phase of the operation.

Zain wondered what images were running around in their heads as the boys were herded down the hill by their mother. They seemed fascinated by the thought of sculpture, but he was unsure that they had a grasp of what sculpture really was. Since the Vasas had move in, Zain had not had any of his pieces around the house. Just before the storm arrived, he had pushed to get everything that was ready for sale into galleries and various places he exhibited. There was no sense in having pieces at home since no one made the trek that far out of town to see them.

The boys kept the clay at the proper humidity. They were much more attentive than he would have been.

The first of the poses Zain chose was a whimsical action where Rose held the end of a towel in her fingertips, The towel hung straight down while Rose executed a lively hip-sprung dance position as if she was moving around a partner. Zain smiled at the elevated little finger on the towel hand. He was reminded of the stereotype of a sophisticate drinking tea.

Zain had to move the sculpture stand out into the shade of the central passageway to get enough light to work. Since he was going to use a Rodinesque surface, he didn't get bogged down in detail. The work went quickly.

By noon the figure was set. When the kids were released for lunch, Erik and Emil made a running detour to the studio to see what they had missed. They came to a skidding halt as they ran past the passageway. Neither had regained their equilibrium before two keening cries were echoing through the hills.

The other kids broke into a run. Bo changed directions to see what was up. Carina stuck her head out the back door to watch. She too headed for the studio after Erik's emphatic wind milling. The Vasa family grouped around the stand as they minutely inspected a rendition of their friend, Rose.

"How'd you do that?" asked Inga.

As the questions came cascading in, Zain suddenly realized that the kids had never made the connection between art and the artist. Art just existed, just as a rock or a hammer existed. They seemed aware that art didn't grow as did a tree or a flower. The best analogy he could think of for such a rudimentary concept was that an artist built a piece of art the same as a carpenter builds a house. They could grasp that concept because they had watched their dad build various rooms on the house and out buildings.

After lunch, Zain turned a critical eye on his first Rose sculpture. It was too static. It didn't adequately portray her essential vitality. He stripped the clay from the waist, hips and towel much to the consternation of Erik and Emil, who had negotiated a ten-minute delay in reporting for their next work assignment.

Zain rolled the stand back to the welding room. He cut the bolt off the left leg and changed the thrust of the hip and the angle of the hip and knee....raising the foot off the ground. To reestablish a two point mounting, he lengthened the rod through the towel and bolted it through the base.

When he put the clay back on the revisited armature, he had a much livelier piece. The hip thrust was accentuated. The weight was shifted enough that the viewer expected the dancer to take another step.

Zain quickly wrapped the clay in a damp cloth and began a second figure. He rather guiltily had to admit to himself that he was showing off to a couple of teenagers. He salved his ego a bit by mentally pointing out that as soon as he heard what the county was going to do and what was left for him and Bo, there would be little time for sculpture. Also, he was going to have to make another food run. This time he'd take the tractor down the valley to the bridge and hitch a ride into town.

That evening, when Erik seriously proclaimed, "Those changes in Rose are much better," Zain had difficulty maintaining the solemnity of the moment. After due conversation, Emil agreed with his brother.

Rose II was a more sedentary pose. Implied motion was replaced by a sense of tension. The left arm was extended straight out as if holding a bow. The towel stretched back to her lips as if she was drawing a bow string. Her feet were planted in a shooting stance. The boys couldn't find room for any improvements.

Zain had one more day he could devote to sculpture, which resulted in two more small pieces wrapped in damp cloths.

The government men arrived the next morning, loaded down with reams of paper. It became a long negotiating session. As time went by, Zain realized that Scott and Martini must be under considerable pressure to bring back a done deal. He was getting concessions he never thought he would see. As the various issues were addressed, it became apparent that the county was the designated negotiator for the state and the feds too.

Both sides of the dining room conference table were happy when the county men climbed into their four-wheel drive vehicle and slithered down the valley. At the dinner table Zain ran down his list of projects. “The county will build a two-way, gravel road from the bridge to the other side of my drive. The county will also maintain the road. Then the state will put in a one-way, with turnouts....on up to the edge of the BLM lands. The feds will take over from that point. There will be a gate at the end of the two-way road to keep the public out.”

Bo broke in. “The county will fence both sides of the road and put in two livestock crossovers. Oh, yes, there will be a bus turnaround at our house. Your mother won’t have to pick you kids up every day.”

“Aw,” said the oldest twins in unison. “What about our bikes?” said Emil.

Carina explained to Zain. Erik and Emil would be going to junior high and they would ride a bus that arrives well after the younger ones. “We said we’d let them ride bikes home.”

“If you guys are going to be helping me in the studio after school and your chores are done, I don’t know if I want you wasting your time peddling home....especially in the winter.”

“You mean it?” demanded Erik.

“Yeah?” said Emil.

“My production has really suffered with this damn storm.

I'm going to have to produce a lot. I also have to do some selling to pay for all this flood expense. We'll have to discuss salary after I see what my expenses are going to be."

"Wow! Money?"

"What I can afford to pay isn't going to make you rich, but maybe you can eventually buy a few goodies or save for college. That's providing your parents approve. Maybe they'd rather you take piano lessons."

"Yuk," said Emil.

"No way," declared Erik.

"I doubt if we could ever get piano lessons to stick," said Carina. "Besides we don't have a piano for practice."

"Oh, there's one in the music room that isn't in use. They could practice there," said Zain with a smirk.

Although the boys read the smile and they knew they were being teased, they still raised a howl of protest, to be on the safe side.

However, Inga and Inger, who had had their heads together, said in unison, "Mom. If we had a piano for practice, we could get lessons in music class."

"Oh, I don't think Zain was serious. He was just teasing your brothers."

Zain shrugged. "Why not? I have no idea when it was last played. It may be horribly out of tune. They'll need to set up a schedule so I can be out in the studio....until they get good."

"Mom, can we? Can we?" pleaded the girls.

"We'll discuss it later," imposed Bo. "There are responsibilities that go along with all these things."

"More immediately," said Zain to cut off the pleading, "in the morning, I'm going to take the tractor down the valley. The county man said the roadway had dried out a lot. I want to see if I can get the van out. We need to make a supply run. Carina, please make a list of food items we need. Bo, if I can get the van out, do you want come along?

If not, make a list of what you need."

"What day will it be? I need to get to the bank. Some checks should be coming in the mail."

Zain checked his watch calendar. Today's Thursday. I'll check the road at first light. If we can drive out, there still will be enough time to go and get back."

Progress was being made toward returning to normalcy. Everyone was more relaxed as the problems were being solved. Everyone went to bed feeling much better.

By the time Zain got back with the tractor from his early morning run, the Vasas had cleared all the sculpture materials out of the van. It was fueled. The ice chests were loaded and Carina's shopping lists were clothes-pinned to the visor.

With a lot of cheering aft, the van rolled down the driveway and began slithering down the valley. After a lot of slipping and sliding but no major perils, Zain and Bo arrived at the county road. Before they could get onto the blacktop, a county bulldozer operator had to make a hole in the berm he'd just thrown up.

As his mud-splattered van bumped onto the county road, Zain said, "We're making good time. I'll drop you off at your bank. As soon as I get through at mine, I'll pick you up."

"Can we go to the post office first? I hope to have some checks to deposit at the bank."

"Sure, no problem. I probably have only bills, but I still need to pick them up. I hate to pay late fees."

It was a whirlwind day as the two men rushed from one store to another. Zain put most of the purchases on his credit card as a matter of convenience. The balances could be sorted out later.

When the van was stuffed with goods and most of the important items were scratched off the list, Zain said, "One more stop. I'll buy you a cup of coffee."

Their destination was Muff's Coffee House. Bo became

a little apprehensive when Zain picked up his laptop and a manila envelope before entering the establishment. Zain marched up to the bar and ordered two cups of black coffee, which came in cups big enough to bathe the kids.

"This won't take long," said Zain, as he set up his computer.

"What are you doing?" asked Bo. He took a sip of his coffee and found strong it enough to suit his pallet.

"I've got to pay some bills. This is a wifi spot. Until we get electricity, I can't go on line. I don't trust that generator to be stable enough to run the computer and the satellite dish."

Bo watched in amazement as Zain flipped through bills. He quickly entered the amounts into the proper spots and moved on. Before Bo's coffee was cool enough to comfortably drink, Zain hit the "pay," command and shut down the computer.

That evening there was ice cream for dessert. Everyone was in a jubilant mood.

"In a couple more days we can probably get our van out," said Bo. "Do you want to take the kids into town?"

"I don't know if I'm up to taking these wild Vikings into civilization," said Carina. "Someone is going to have to watch them all the time or they'll be running around naked, plundering the citizenry."

"Aw, mom," came a cry in unison.

"We're going to have to get them tamed down in a hurry," said Bo. "Won't be long until school starts."

Another negative cry went up.

Bo continued. "We have a lot to do before our work force disappears all day long." That shed another light on the situation. The kids got to thinking school might not be that bad an idea after all.

Zain changed the subject. "In case anyone is interested, I'm going to weld up some more armatures early in the morning."

"Can we help?" cried Erik and Emil.

"If you get up early enough. I hope to be finished before breakfast."

"Dad, will you get us up in the morning?"

"Sure, but I'll only call you once."

"We'll get up."

"I need four more of the two-foot armatures. I'm also going to start a bigger figure. Do you want to cut the rods this evening so they will be ready to weld in the morning?"

"Sure."

"Okay. This one will be four feet from the top of the head to the heels. Use the back photo with the stick figure. Compute your factor of increase and then draw the big figure on the concrete with the chalk. Then you can just lay the rod on the lines and mark the length. Use the bolt cutters to cut the steel. Cut the rods for the two-foot armatures, too. The marks are already on the floor."

As soon as the boys could escape their kitchen chores, they were out of the house. Zain let them flail away for an hour before staging a rescue.

Two frustrated thirteen-year old were sniping at each other as Zain approached the welding shop. He remained out of sight long enough to determine the problem....fractions.

"How're you coming?" asked Zain as he stepped into the shop.

"Oh boy, this is tough," wailed Emil. "How exact do these have to be?"

"Don't get sloppy on the first step. You've got to get everything as right as you can get it if you expect to have a successful piece. There's no sense in starting if you're not going to do your best. Your best and my best will be different in many respects but there should be one common denominator....the piece should be our best at that given time. What's your problem?"

"That factor thing."

"You forgot what I told you. Convert to metrics."

The twins glowered at each other for not remembering.

Zain relieved Emil of the steel tape. He drew out four feet and read the metric side of the tape, "122cm." Then he measured the overall height of the stick figure drawn on the print. "21.4." He picked up the calculator from the desk. "122 divided by 21.4 is 5.7. That's your factor. He handed the tape back to Emil. "Have fun." Zain returned to the house for another cup of coffee.

Half an hour later, the twins triumphantly entered the kitchen all puffed up with success. "Once you get the hang of it....no problem," announced Erik.

"That's good, dears," said Carina. "Now it's bed time. And don't you dare wake the little ones again.."

"Aw, mom," came the standard reply.

In the morning, Zain fussed around the studio doing little jobs until the boys finally arrived. Their mom had fortified them with orange juice and a slice of bread to hold them until breakfast.

The fog of sleep vanished when Zain handed the twins welding goggles and then fired up the oxygen/acetylene torch. The sculptor gave a running commentary of each step along the way, plus constant safety admonitions.

He welded all the stick figures. Referring to the Rose photos, he bent the shafting to match the action. Next, bolts were attached to the points that would make contact with the base.

After he welded the steel for the big figure and bent the rod into the action position, Zain said, "This armature isn't strong enough to hold up the weight of the clay. It has to be reinforced. We'll do that this evening. Let's get some breakfast."

Carina must have been watching. When the guys came through the back door, the big stove griddle was loaded with pancakes ready to flip. By the time Zain and the boys had washed off the shop grime, Bo was there with the fresh milk. A great platter of hot pancakes and a pitcher of hot, homemade syrup arrived simultaneously with the hungry males.

"How about taking the tractor down the valley?" said Bo. "I want to pick up some of that lumber that washed away. I'm going to make frames to hold plastic sheeting to cover those broken windows until I can get some new glass. As soon as we get electricity we can move back into our house."

"Sure, take the tractor. While you're down there, check with the county. As soon as they run a blade through the narrows, we'll be able to come and go in the vans without getting an adrenaline high."

The conversation was interrupted by the keening alert. A stern look from Bo held the boys in their places. Carina ushered Scott and Martini, along with their mugs of coffee, into the dining room. The county men declined the offer of breakfast.

"We've got a bunch of papers to sign," said Scott.

With a couple of hand signs, Bo signaled Erik and Emil to clear the table and dismissed them.

Scott continued. "All we discussed has been translated into legalese. There are a few minor changes so it would work out. We'll go over them with you. Also you might be interested to know that the phone company is going to run a line to the dam sites along the power right-of-way on your back property line. They'll make a drop at the same place the power company will put your hook-up."

"Great," said Zain.

"There's a down-side to that. You'll have to bring the lines in yourself and those hills only have a shallow ground cover over granite. You'll never drill post holes in it."

"We'll make tripod frames," said Zain. "I have the poles

to do that."

Before all the paperwork was understood and signed, Carina served sandwiches.

After the county men left, there was still enough time for Bo to go foraging. Zain headed for the welding studio to lay out the materials needed to strengthen the large armature. As Zain buzzed around collecting items, he suddenly realized he was setting the stage to show off again in front of a couple of teenagers. He'd been deluding himself by claiming to be anxious to start on the large Rose sculpture. Oh, that desire was there too, but the unnecessary exercise of laying out materials belied that as the major reason. Zain shook his head as he continued to prepare for the demonstration. He decided that trying to show youngsters a new world wasn't a bad thing. Maybe some of it would stick.

The demonstration had to wait for another day because Bo and the twins didn't get back until almost dark.

As soon as the tractor came to a halt, Emil jumped off the loaded trailer. "Looky what we got," he yelled before keen-calling the rest of the family.

Bo dismounted, stretched and stood for a moment trying to figure out a way of telling what had happened without it sounding as if he was bragging. Instead of saying anything, he pulled Carina up close and let the boys tell the story.

Erik wasn't opposed to bragging. "Look at all the wire we got. We went clear to the bridge. There was a lot of our wire in the debris dam. It was holding all that stuff together. When dad started to pull it loose, the guys came over to help."

"It was a real mess," injected Emil. "I don't think those guys wanted to work that hard."

"You can't say that young man," admonished Bo. "They didn't realize what they were getting into," said Bo with a lopsided grin. "That stuff was really tangled up."

"One of the bosses went over to the electrical guys who were stringing wire across the river. When he came back, he said that the road guys and the power guys figured it would be a lot easier and cheaper to give us new wire than giving us the time to salvage our wire out of that mess. One of the bulldozers made a ramp so we could get the tractor up by the bridge."

Emil picked up the story. "The power company back hoe lifted a spool off the truck and put it on our trailer. Dad says there's enough here to get electricity to the house."

"Great," said Zain, with feeling. "Recovering that wire would take a lot of time and sweat."

Bo turned to his wife. "With that ramp up to the road, our old van can make it through. How'd you like to take the kids into town, have a lunch you don't have to cook, do some shopping and get the mail?"

A great cheer went up. The kids found new sources of energy to cavort about until they got down to the serious discussion of where they should have their "first meal." Carina laughingly accepted the consensus view to McDonalds would be as far removed from their recent fare as possible.

"We'll all go in, but I'll drop off at truck row," said Bo. "I have to get another farm truck. We have a lot of stuff to haul."

For the first time in what seemed like a century, Zain was alone.....well, not quite alone. Every time he crossed the yard, Matilda, the pot bellied pig wanted affection. Also an assorted gaggle of fowl followed in his wake. He had to improvise a gate to keep the birds from crapping all over his studio as they followed him right in the door.

With his uninterrupted time, Zain started packing clay on the large armature. At that point in the process, little effort was made to create form other than basic proportion. As the figure developed, Zain made adjustments. He put a little more arch in the back changing the balance slightly. The viewer was given the distinct impression that the girl was about to take a step to maintain balance. Zain felt the implied action gave life to his work.

Late in the afternoon, a bunch of well-spent kids stumbled out of their old van next to the back porch. But, Carina was still going strong as she directed the unloading and distribution of new supplies.

It was almost dark when a vintage stake-truck pulled into the Vasa yard. A sizeable load of building supplies was stacked on the back. Bo parked his new acquisition in the barn before trekking up the hill.

For everyone, the next few days were just blurs. Work went on at a frantic rate. During the days, Zain and Bo erected tripod poles to carry the electrical wire until they got close to the houses where the soil cover became deep enough to hold poles. It would be a time to celebrate when lights went on in both houses. With lights and power to run the tools, construction could go on well into the night. And Zain could work in his studio at any hour of the night or day.

Bo had spent much of his $1000 grant from the building supplier to buy paneling. The emphasis was on putting wall coverings on before appliances and furniture were moved back into the lower reaches. Open spaces could be covered at leisure.

Carina had work crews cleaning Zain's house as well as her own. Erik and Emil alternately worked with the men and provided supervision for the younger ones. Inga and Inger were put in charge of getting all the barnyard animals back home. Moving the feeding places down the hill provided the needed incentives.

Zain worked as much as he could on the large sculpture. It was progressing as he had envisioned it. As he worked his thoughts invariably turned toward Rose. The same was apparently true for Erik and Emil. As he was putting the final touches on the face, both boys were perched on stools watching intently.

When Zain stepped back to examine his efforts, Erik said, "That doesn't look like Rose."

"How so?" said Zain.

"Nose is too straight."

"And?"

"The lips are too big."

"And?"

"It's a pretty face," said Emil, "just like Frances."

"Who's Frances?" said Zain.

"Oh, there's another set of twins at school. Frances is really good looking. Her sister's not ugly, but nowhere as cute as Fran."

"But, all the boys like Freddie better than Fran," said Erik in his usual declarative manner.

"You're right," said Zain. I don't want people to look at this piece and say, 'Oh, I know her. That's Rose. I just want a pleasant face that adds appeal to the sculpture."

"I wonder if Rose got the rest of her tattoo." said Erik.

Still having some mixed feeling on the subject of tattooing, Zain said, "I hope she did. It was very important to her."

"Do you think she'll ever come back?" Emil looked off into the distance with a pensive expression. "I like her."

"She didn't say," said Zain."It would be nice to see her again." To himself he said, "Maybe next time I won't be such a klutz. She was probably glad to get out of this nut house. Why would she come back?"

Chapter 11

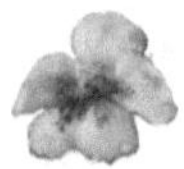

Bo was driving his truck and Zain was riding beside him. They had just been to the back property line to turn on the electricity. Their newly strung line was hot. When they got back down the hill, they would throw the switches to electrify their houses.

That would be a momentous occasion. The Vasas were poised to reoccupy their house. Most of their belongings had already been shuffled downhill. If the electric range worked, Carina would cook dinner in her own kitchen. And Zain was going to have to go back to fending for himself.

Summer was winding down. The schools would open soon.

When Bo switched off the engine, they could hear the helicopter but they couldn't see it against the early morning sun. The kids started popping up from their work assignments.

"That's the TV helicopter," called eagle-eye Erik.

The machine hovered over the valley and slowly rotated as if scanning the course of the river. Then it moved over the

Vasa house and on to Zain's. Those on the ground could see the cameraman taking his shots and Hunter talking in the mike.

Finally, the machine settled down on its former landing spot. Hunter hopped out. His photographer delayed long enough to take some shots of the kids in their gray gym clothes.

"Hi, Bo, Zain," yelled Hunter as he advanced with an extended hand. "The brass wants a follow-up on flood victims. Things have certainly changed since I was last out here. The water was still up in the house. I see you're getting a new road. Is everything about back to normal?"

"Can't say it's back to normal," said Zain, "but it's a lot better." When we throw the switch over on that pole, and if the house doesn't burn down, Bo will sleep in his own bed tonight."

"Now you can watch Channel 6. The boss wants a follow-up on the Vasa family. I'm glad to accommodate him because I wanted to get back out here. When I get finished down below I want to talk to you."

"Oh, really?"

"Yeah, but later. Bo can we see what happened to the interior of your house? From the pile of debris it looks as if there was a lot of damage."

Zain gave a wave of his hand. "Go ahead, Bo. I'm going to turn the electricity on in the barns and studio before I try the houses." Zain headed for the box they'd mounted on a pole.

An hour later, Zain was luxuriating in an abundance of light in his studio. Hunter found him checking the clay humidity. He was without his cameraman for once.

"Hey Zain, have you heard from Rose?"

"Not a word. Of course, I don't have a phone and the mail has been problematical. Have you?"

Hunter shot him a quizzical glance. "I never really expected to. I got the distinct impression that she was already taken. All she did was talk about you. If it wasn't you, then it was the Vasa kids. I never got a chance to make my own case."

Zain laughed. "Rose faked you out. We didn't have anything going. I think she was more than happy to get out of here. She was anxious to get to Seattle."

"Not all that anxious. When we got back to town, we stopped for a fast food lunch. I had to get back to the station. I tried to get her to hang around until after the 6:00 o'clock news. I invited her to out for dinner and drinks later, but she gave me to understand that she couldn't run around behind your back. She had me drop her off at the bus station. Later, I found out she stayed in town a couple more days over at the art school."

Hunter took on a hurt look. "Don't feel badly," said Zain with a chuckle. "You were dealing with a really smart cookie. She ends up doing just exactly what she wants."

The newsman shook off his personal feeling and went back into his professional mode. "You may not have had anything going, but Rose is certainly a fan. She bent my ear all during lunch on what a good sculptor you were. She told me which galleries handled your work. Last week I made the rounds. I'm no art critic, but I think she's right. You're good."

"Thanks," said Zain as he wondered where this was going.

"Rose also said you were planning a series featuring her. Have you started any of them yet?"

"With all the flood problems I haven't had much time, but I've gotten a little work done."

"May I see it?"

"It's just in clay."

"Great. I'd like to do a little feature on you as a local artist. That would be educational as well as entertaining." Hunter was getting energized just thinking about the project.

Zain was a little skeptical of Hunter and his possibly self-centered motives, but an artist lives or dies on publicity. Zain's two shadows materialized at the studio door.

"Can we show him?" cried an eager Erik.

"We'll be careful." added Emil.

As the first of the small pieces was unveiled, Hunter said, "I've got to get my cameraman," as he charged out the door.

While the newsman was away, Zain set up the scene. He shoved the model stand off into a corner. The boys pushed the wheeled sculpture stand into the focal spot of the flood lights. By the time the reporter returned, the stage was set. Zain was in charge. Hunter didn't have a chance. He stepped into the lights next to Zain and a clay figure. After a brief introduction, Hunter asked the sculptor a procedural question. Zain started a running commentary. As soon as he had described one piece, a cute teenage boy dress only in a pair of gray gym shorts moved it out of the way only to have it replaced by a duplicate teenager. Then Erik wheeled in the larger piece. The two boys dropped to the floor so they could slowly rotate the stand.

Zain had kept his comments brief and the exchanges crisp, making the segment difficult to cut. Hunter was left to make a quick exit.

Ruefully, Hunter said, "Next time I'll just hand you the mike and I won't have to be a mike stand." Although he'd lost the spot light, he knew he had a good tight piece that he knew he could sell to his boss.

After the news helicopter departed, Zain and Bo checked the electrical hookups at the Vasa farm. Everything worked. Bo switched on his immersible pump to begin clearing his well. The family swarmed over the house, readying it for the move the next day.

Carina cooked her last dinner in Zain's kitchen, but this

time on the electric range. She had a work crew cleaning utensils and polishing lamp shades. All the emergency equipment was going back into storage.

Dinner preparations were put on hold so everyone could see the six o'clock news. Early in the program was the piece on the Vasas. The females moaned and groaned over their stringy hair and unkempt appearances. The boys laughed at their stoic, straight-backed father. But, the whole family felt proud of their success in turning a disaster into a victory. Carina added her own remarks making certain each of her kids received praise for their contributions. She also included Zain in her comments. The kids would not let him shrug them off.

Near the end of the broadcast was the piece on Zain. Hunter had gone to the effort of filming a couple of his bronzes in a local gallery. Zain was pleased with the PR. At the conclusion of the piece Zain said, "Not bad, but do you know who will glean the biggest benefit?"

There was nearly a unanimous, "Who?"

"My two young helpers. I'll bet the phones are ringing right now. Within hours every junior high school girl will know about those two cute boys in skimpy gym shorts who are assistants in a sculpture studio."

Erik and Emil immediately turned red. Carina rolled her eyes to the ceiling, "Oh, no."

"It's a good thing you don't live in town," said Zain. "The sidewalks would be crowded with teenage girls hoping to glimpse them. Every time they mowed the lawn, you'd have a crowd control problem."

Even Bo laughed at the image Zain was painting. Inga and Inger weren't quite old enough to figure out what all the fuss was about, but they enjoyed the discomfort of their big brothers.

There were only a few days before Zain's theory could be tested. School was about to start. There was a flurry of activity in the Vasa house getting school clothes sorted out. This year, due to the flood, there would be fewer new, stylish statements. Elen and Elsa were about to make their school debut.

Zain now spent most of his time in the studio. After school, Erik and Emil were permitted to work a couple of hours in the studio before dinner and homework. It worked out well, since that was also the piano practice time for the two older girls in the music room.

There was a subtle change in Zain's life. Since the flood notoriety and his more public entry in to local art scene, weekends were becoming informal open houses.. Hunter was the first visitor. Actually, on that occasion, he was trying to impress a svelte Saturday night date with his cultural acumen. Any guy could take his date to the movies, or a play at the local college, but it took someone special to gain access to a working art studio in a glorious, old mansion.

Zain was heading for the house for a cup of coffee when he noticed a plume of dust coming down the road at a high rate of speed. Zain expected it to be a carload of kids who would come to a slithering stop at the county gate. They would turn around in his driveway and roar back in the other direction. Fortunately, the prevailing winds usually carried the dust down the valley instead of up to his house.

However, the little red sports car whipped into his driveway and cut Zain off at the back door. There was a whir of the window regulator and Hunter Hawk's face appeared as the tinted glass disappeared into the slot.

"Hi, Zain. How'd you like that piece I did on you? The station got a lot of good feed-back. So did the Vasa piece."

Not waiting for an answer, Hunter popped out of the car and hurried around to the passenger side to be a gentleman and open the door for his companion. "Come on, Britney. Let me introduce you to our eminent sculptor."

A very striking blond made an amazingly graceful exit from the cramped confines of Hunter's muscle car. The bright smile slipped somewhat as she surveyed the rural scene of stable, barn and dry brown hills. It dulled even further as a clay besmudged figure extended a not-too-clean hand.

An unenthusiastic "Hello" was accompanied by a momentary, fingertip handshake.

Zain received the distinct impression that Britney was in the wrong place at the wrong time of day. She exhibited all the signs of being a nocturnal city dweller.

"I was just heading in to get a cup of coffee," said Zain. "Would you care to join me?'

"I've got a better idea," said Hunter. He went to the trunk to get a six-pack of Guiness from an ice chest. "Got some glasses?"

"Let's see what we can find." Zain let the way through the mud room into the kitchen. For a moment he paused to decide if he'd go to the cabinets holding the peanut jar mugs or the crystal. He decided not to intentionally sabotage Hunter's amorous efforts. He pulled down three crystal tumblers and led the way to the front parlor.

Britney exhibited much more interest in her surroundings as she passed down the great hall, past the enormous dining room, the library and the music room.

As the trio settled into easy chairs, Zain commented, "You're in luck. Things aren't normally this clean, but before the Vasas moved back to their house, Carina had the whole crew give this place a first class cleaning. Enjoy it while it lasts. I run a vacuum cleaner and dust mop through about once a month."

"You live here by yourself?" asked Britney.

"The Vasa family was here because of the flood, but normally it's only Wolf, Nutsy and me."

"Who?"

"The cat and the dog," said Hunter, with a laugh. "Wait until you see the cat. He was in one of the shots, Mike, my cameraman took on my first trip out here. My boss made me cut it out. He thought it was too graphic."

"What's wrong with the cat?"

As Hunter started to respond, Zain said, "Oh, don't spoil the fun. Let her find out for herself."

Britney's lower lip popped out. She fell silent, but her eyes continued to appraise her surroundings.

About that time a minor whirlwind came racing down the hall. Inga and Inger peeled off into the music room.

"It's time to head for the studio," said Zain, "unless you want to listen to a couple of very loud beginning pianists."

"Can I see the music room?" asked Britney.

"I'll introduce you to the girls."

It was still warm enough for the girls to be in their gym shirts. They were perched on the piano bench, each doing scales an octave apart on a grand piano which rewarded enthusiasm. Zain had to walk around in front of them to get their attention. As the clamor died away, both girls began to apologize. They thought the visitors would be in the studio.

Britney's eyes skimmed the room. There was no sign of recognition as her gaze passed over the plaster bust of Bach, Beethoven and Mozart. The various cased stringed instruments scattered around the room held no interest for her. "Don't you have a keyboard?"

"When this room was built and furnished, the guy who invented the keyboard probably hadn't been born yet," quipped Zain, who was beginning to realize how shallow the water was in Britney's pond. "The most modern instrument in here is a Solovox, an early electronic devise. I took it off the piano to avoid distraction. Get on with your practice, girls. We're going to the studio."

"I'll get the Guiness," said Hunter as he headed for the

parlor.

It immediately became apparent that Britney was not going to be any more comfortable in the studio than she was in the traditional music room. She shied away from any clay residue or dust as if it was anthrax powder.

Hunter became aware that he had selected the wrong itinerary to impress his date. He rolled his eyes to the ceiling as he stashed the Guinesses in the studio refrigerator.

"Gosh, I lost track of time," said Hunter. "We'd better hurry or we'll miss Happy Hour at the Bix. Want to come along, Zain?"

"No thanks, I see my two apprentices are lurking about outside. I have to put them to work."

As Hunter herded Britney across the yard to his car, he shouted, "I still want to see your new pieces."

"Any time."

As the car tracked up the dirt road back toward town, Erik said, "What was that all about?"

Zain figured that the boys wouldn't understand the boy-impress-girl routine. Besides, sex education should be left to their parents.

Instead, Zain said, "She didn't want to get dirty. That tells me that this place needs a good cleaning. I don't want to drive any more potential customers away."

The next visitor turned out to be a real client. The following Sunday, another car came wheeling into the yard. This time it pulled up in front of the house. The visitors were Judge Winters and his wife Pamela.

Zain met the judge coming up the steps.

"Hi Judge. So nice to see you." He stepped forward to shake hands.

"My wife wanted me to check if it would be possible to see your studio."

"Sure, come on in."

The judge trotted back to the car to help his wife and new

baby out of the car. He opened the rear door to release his little son from his safety seat.

The new mother adjusted the baby in her chest carrier and advanced with her hand out. "Zain, it is so nice to see you out from under the shadow of impending disaster."

"Mrs. Winters," said Zain as he shook hands. "I have to apologize. I have been remiss in not more adequately thanking you for all the kindnesses you showed us during the flood."

"First, call me Pam. Secondly, no thanks are necessary. We were glad to do it, even if as a result of our minor participation, we hadn't become the focal point of our social circle," Pam laughed merrily.

"None-the-less, we really appreciated you assistance. Thank you," said Zain, as he bent over to get a better look at the newborn. "And who do we have here?"

"Dats Molly," declared her little brother, Jeffy, in his most authoritative voice.

Everyone laughed. The judge tousled his son's hair and pulled the child up against his leg.

Pamela charged on. "We didn't know there was a wonderful house like this in the area until Hawk did that piece on you. And then to have a working studio too."

The judge broke in. "What this is all about is that my wife is dying to see your house. Our social crowd expects us to know all about it since we are neighbors and we know you. As for me, I'd like to see your studio."

Pam faked a kick at the judge's shin. "He never lets me talk."

"That's because you take such a circuitous route. I have to interpret."

Zain laughed. "Beware, I only clean house with two weeks notice. He led the way up the steps to the front door. Pam oohed and awed her way through each room. The dual kitchen fascinated her and the multiple bathroom brought peels of laughter. The judge saw possibilities in the cavernous basement game room.

"Okay," said the judge. "Dear, you've gotten the celebrity tour of the house. Now, Zain, could we see your studio?"

"Sure. Let's go through the kitchen so I can put on the coffee pot. It'll be ready by the time we get through the studio."

On the way to the studio, Erik and Emil miraculously appeared.

As Zain started introductions, Pam said, "Oh, I recognize these two and even with clothes on. They were in Hawk's feature on the studio."

Both boys blushed furiously. Pam blithely continued on. "I hear they lead the popularity parade with all the girls at the junior high school."

Zain came to the twins' rescue. "Go unwrap the last three pieces and yours too." To gain a little time after the boys fled to the studio, Zain pointed out some of the interesting features of the area such as the old carriage house, the new power line and the high water mark on the Vasa house.

By the time they got into the studio, two smaller clay pieces were sitting on stands under the lights. A large figure, which had its own wheels was standing in the middle. Zain had trained the boys how to show pieces to their best advantages. They also knew to turn to the wall the plywood sheets on which the nude model photos were tacked.

"Oh, my," said Pam.

The judge didn't say anything, but he immediately scooped up his son to keep little fingers out of soft clay.

"These are of Rose?" asked Pam. "The bodies are hers but the face on the big one is different."

"The boys caught me on that with the first one. I put generic faces on my pieces unless I'm commissioned to do a portrait. I don't want people to be able to say, 'Oh, I saw you naked at a friend's house'."

"Good plan," said the judge. "I can imagine a case of a guy trying to sue you when he finds a nude sculpture of his brand new wife in the local gallery window. Where are you going with this series?"

"I'd like to be able to mount a major exhibition of the Lady with the Towel. Depending on the sizes, I figure I'd need twenty-five pieces."

"That's a sizeable investment at the price of bronze work these days."

"It sounds as if you have some familiarity with the art scene."

"He's a member of the board for the local museum," said Pam. "He researches everything he does."

"These aren't going to be unique pieces are they?"

"No. I plan to cast an artist's proof and a series of eight. I can't afford to do solo pieces even when I don't send the work to an outside foundry."

"Do you do the whole thing?"

"Usually, but I hate to make molds. On a project of this size I'll bring in a guy I know to help. He's a master mold maker until the sun starts to drop in the west. A regular job interferes with his pleasures. I give him a room, feed him, keep the refrigerator full of beer and give him a few bucks when the job is done.

"For heavy casting, I bring in some help. To get bodies, all I have to do is put a notice on the art school bulletin board that I need help casting and I have all the help I can use. When my two apprentices muscle up a little bit, they can handle the other end of the pouring cradle."

Pam turned her attention to Erik and Emil, who were lurking outside of the bright floodlights. "Oh yes, our two heartthrobs"

Both boys again turned red.

"Dear," said the judge. "Have a heart. That's a very tender

subject at this age."

Zain stepped into the flood lights to push his two small sculptures out of the center. He motioned the boys to move their pieces in. "Independent of their looks, wait until you see what they can do. Come on guys, uncover them."

The boys removed the damp rags to reveal two full male figures the same size of the small Rose sculptures.

"The boys are using each other as models."

The technique there were using was about midway between the free flowing style Zain was using on the small pieces and the nearly full representative style he was employing on the larger figures.

The judge stepped forward to get a closer look. "Hey, guys, these are really impressive. Good work."

"You'd better not let the girls as school see these or you'll really get some notoriety," said the judge's wife.

"Pam," warned her husband rather sharply.

"I'm just having some fun. Erik, Emil, those pieces are great. And remember, there's nothing wrong with being good looking and having talent too."

The judge rolled his eyes.

Zain motioned for the boys to put the pieces away. "Let's have a cup of coffee." Looking at Pamela he asked, "In which room would you like to sit?"

"Oh, the library. I want to check out the books," said Pamela as she shifted the baby for easier walking and headed for the door.

Under normal conditions, Zain would have put three mugs on a plastic tray and poured the coffee from a thermal carafe. But Pamela Winters was collecting tales to tell her friends. He stepped into the formal dining room to collect a silver coffee service and matching tray. Zain stopped short of a full formal service by putting Jeffy's orange juice into a plastic cup instead of crystal.

When the tray was loaded, Zain led the way to the library.

The judge juggled the chairs at a library table into a more intimate grouping while Zain served.

Pam stayed seated long enough to sample the coffee. "Oh, This is good, but different. What is it?"

"It's southern coffee with chicory."

"Umm," said Pam as she took another sip. Then she unhooked the baby and handed Molly to her father. "I don't want to climb ladders with her. Zain won't tell if you hold the baby."

"Judge?" said Zain.

"First, call me Ray and second there are some people who would think it unseemly for a judge to lower himself to domestic pursuits.

"When you're a judge, everyone either wants to garner favor or at least stay on your good side by showing respect. At home and in my neighborhood I'd like not to be continually reminded of my job. When we're in an informal setting, please call me Ray."

From her lofty perch at the top of the ladder, Pam said, "Ray is a district court judge now, but the various powers around the county consider him to be the leading candidate for the next circuit court opening. That's why everyone is so respectful. At the same time, the steering powers want to keep him squeaky clean and not found doing anything unjudge-like."

"Oh, come on. It's not that bad."

"Oh, look," squealed Pam, "French and German."

"Most of the books," said Zain, "were bought by the pound. However, old man Graff was originally from Alsace-Lorraine, so he had a few pounds of French and German books added. From the looks of most of the books, they have never been read."

"Pam was a French major in college," said Ray.

"You can borrow anything you like. Both the older twins seemed to favor mysteries. The other side of the room is mostly who-done-its."

"That's more my speed, " said Ray. "Zain, I'd like to place an order for one of eight of the girl stomping on the end of the towel. I get the feeling she planted that foot with real authority. From what I know of Rose, that is a real reflection of her personality."

"It will be a while before I start casting any of the series."

"That's all right....when it gets done. I'll give you a deposit before I leave. I'd like to see the big figures when they're done. I have a perfect niche for one of them.

"Another thing. Do you suppose you could get the boys to each do a figure that relates to the other so that they can put both on the same base? I'd like to be their first client."

"That's an interesting concept. Wow, I can see all sorts of ramifications for the twins. Let me work on that."

"I like both of those figures that they are doing. Have you helped them or is it their own work?"

Zain laughed. "Every time I get my hand on their work you can probably hear their wails clear down to the highway. When something isn't right, I pinch off the offending clay. I also kill all sacred cows."

"Sacred cows?"

"A sacred cow is a beautifully executed part that doesn't fit into its surroundings. Yesterday Erik sculpted a very good right foot and ankle, but it was too big to fit the rest of the figure. You should have heard the cries of anguish. You'd have thought that I was pinching off his own right foot. They're good kids and they are learning fast."

Pam rejoined the group, collected Molly and checked on Jeffy, who had fallen asleep with his head on his father's foot. After taking a drink of her cold coffee, she asked, "Where is Rose?

"I haven't heard from her. Of course, I'm still without a phone."

"Is she comeing back?"

"I have no idea."

"Have you tried to get in contact with her?"

"Pam, you're getting terribly personal," said Ray.

"They made such a nice looking couple. I'd hate to see them lose one another."

"It's not your business."

"That's all right, Ray. I have no way of getting in contact with her. She doesn't have a permanent address and I don't even know her full name. I suspect that 'Rose' is probably a nickname. I've been so busy with storm damage and getting this new series together, I haven't had time to give her much thought," he lied. He didn't want to admit even to himself how often Rose had passed through his thoughts. He had tried to rationalize that it was because he was working with her images all around. But, his thoughts and visualizations bore little relationship to images offered by the photographs.

Zain continued lamely, "I plan to take a short break after making the molds and pulling the waxes. Maybe I'll make some inquiries."

The judge rolled his eyes and changed the subject. "I have a few friends in the art world. How long would you need to mount a major show?

"My next show will be all Rose bronzes. It's going to take about two years' work. Of course, that's predicated on there being sufficient money. There are considerable expenses involved, even when I'm doing my own work. And also there is the problem of eating while I'm doing it. I'll have to do some selling along the line."

"From what I've seen, you shouldn't have any problem placing a show in a first class location. If I leave a $2,000 deposit on that Rose sculpture, will that help feed you for a while?"

"It certainly will. Thank you."

The judge pulled a check book from his hip pocket and wrote a check. As he slid it across the table, he said, "Let me know if the boys will cooperate on a piece. That should be interesting."

Ray collected his son off the floor. Pam handed Molly to him long enough for her to run up the ladder to collect a couple of French books.

After the Winters' car rolled down the driveway, Zain returned to the studio. The boys were making busywork more to avoid going home to chores than straighten the work space.

"Hey, guys. You can put a star on Rose stomping on the towel. The judge just gave me a deposit on #1."

"Wow!" cried the twins in unison.

"You mean he bought it before it's made?" said Emil.

"Sure. There's nothing strange about that. Your dad had to put a deposit at the hospital before you were born."

"That's not the same thing," said Emil with a humph.

"Well, you're right. The judge could see what he is getting before the actual event. Your dad had to take whatever came out."

"Aw," came a duet wail.

"Well, maybe your dad got more than he bargained for," said Zain. While the twins were figuring out how to take that comment, Zain continued."Would you guys check the school library tomorrow to see if they have any books with a lot of good pictures on Greco-Roman wrestling?"

"What's that?" said Emil.

"It's a kind of wrestling they do in college," said Erik.

"It's also an Olympic sport," said Zain.

CHAPTER 12

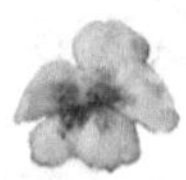

Pam Winters' inquiries about Rose had again raised a mountain of unanswered questions in Zain's mind. It might have been some solace if he'd known that he was not alone in his uncertainties.

After that impromptu kiss that she had laid on Zain, Rose quickly hopped aboard the helicopter to cover a host of mixed feelings that threatened to erupt. She didn't understand her reason for such a bold action. Since she'd made the decision to leave, she had continually been telling herself that it was the right thing to do. There were things to be done that couldn't wait. The tattoo was the most important item on her schedule. It had to be finished. Blade was dying. She couldn't hang around any longer.

However, in the broad scheme of things, a few days weren't going to make that much difference. The uncomfortable sin of selfishness was pricking her. The Vasas had just gone through a disaster. Sure, she'd helped a bit by ginning-up the bleeding hearts for a needed relief effort. She still couldn't understand Bo's resistance and Zain's obvious lack of enthusiasm. It must have something to do with that bloody machoism that males hail as a virtue.

But, the real enigma that was bothering her was Zain. She thought she had rubbed shoulders with the full gamut of sexual persuasions, but he didn't match any she'd come across. There had to be something else there. She should have hung around long enough to find out.

Her line of thought was broken by Hunter, who had satisfied all of his professional requirements. Now he was ready to turn his attention to getting laid. Rose hung a smile on her face, commencing a long, intricate mating dance in which she knew she would prevail. In the end, Hunter Hawk would be frustrated but not sufficiently displeased to cause her any problems. He would probably remain a friend.

After disposing of Hunter, Rose decided to stay in town a while longer. She still had some unanswered questions. She found a shelter and then headed for the school. Devon shifted things around so she could get in a couple of days work. That gave her ample time to grill the sculpture instructor about Zain. Information was scant, but she learned that Zain maintained a strict professional decorum with his models.....male or female. He dated girls and there was no suspicion of him being gay.

Rose had hoped that finding out more about Zain would make her feel better, but the more she heard, the worse she felt. The problem must be with her.

The trip to Seattle was not nearly as enjoyable as she normally found cross-country travel. Most of her time was spent in self-examination, looking for flaws that had obviously turned off a good-looking guy. Try as she might, Rose couldn't find any disqualifying personal traits. She had always considered herself a caring person, willing to help anyone in need. Untold hours had been spent in community service, protests against injustice, and rallies for worthy causes.

When Seattle was the next bus stop, Rose finally had to admit that the problem was probably the tattoo. She had been resisting that conclusion through two states. The tattoo was nothing she could change or eliminate, even if she had wanted to. Besides, it meant too much to her. It was a living tribute to her mother, whom she had not sufficiently honored in life. Also the designing and painting of the tattoo was her creative apex. No, if the problem was the tattoo she would have to look elsewhere for a more understanding guy. It was a shame. Zain had so many interesting facets. He had real possibilities for a fine mate.... both physically and intellectually.

As Rose had done on several earlier occasions, she snapped her mind shut on the Zain interlude. Shouldering her backpack, she stepped off the bus into a new world untainted by disturbing thoughts. The day was bright and shiny. She ignored all the unsavories who haunted the terminal, and she strode off into a new adventure.

Blade lived in the country. She would catch a bus as far as she could and then hitch a ride the rest of the way. Blade would have driven in to the city to pick her up, but she didn't know how he was feeling, and besides, she, wanted to greet him without the whole world watching. Theirs was a special relationship. No one in the world knew more about Rose than Blade, and she felt comfortable with that knowledge. Of course, she also knew as much about Blade as anyone, which put her into a very select club.

The last ride dropped her off at a mailbox. A gravel road led off into the trees. It was a good hike to get to the farmhouse. The scene was very rural....a two-story farmhouse with a large veranda along two sides. Behind the house was a long, low stable and a big red barn beyond that.

Rose gave a knowing smile as she scanned the area. Outside of an occasional new board here and a splash of fresh paint there, the farm looked the same as when she first saw it over four years ago. The operation was not as bucolic as it appeared on the surface. The horse stalls in the stables had been turned into recovery rooms. The central hallway was a common area with a library, TV and ancillary electronics. At the far end was a large freezer of dinners and snacks next to a phalanx of microwave ovens. There was also a refrigerator full of non-alcoholic beverages.

The barn was used mostly for out-of-sight parking.

The old farmhouse appeared to be on post and pillar. Actually, beneath was a sizeable basement beneath that was the heart of the operation....the surgery.

As Rose mounted the step onto the porch, she shed her knapsack and dropped it beside the door before she twisted the ancient rachet bell in the door. Under normal circumstances, she would have been ready to launch herself into Blade's big, burly arms. But word of her friend's illness made her rethink that greeting. When Blade opened the door, Rose was shocked and, oh, so glad to have opted for a different greeting. The only thing that was the same was the broad grin that spread across his face. Physically, Blade was a mere shadow of his former self. Instead of a stocky, well-muscled block of a man, a wasted figure in oversized clothes stood before her.

Blade stepped forward to initiate an enveloping hug, minus their traditional, smooching kiss. They'd been special friends for a long time. Rose battled back tears as she clung to him like a morning glory.

Finally, Blade swung her away and patted the right hip. "Ready to fill that final blank?"

"You bet. Wait until you see my last painting."

Rose scooped up her knapsack before Blade got to it. "Don't," he said to her as he took it away from her and led the way into the kitchen. He selected a couple of mugs from the mugtree, gave each a measure of his special coffee extract and drew boiling water from another spigot.

When the two faced each other across the kitchen table, Rose was battling tears. Blade reached across the table to take Rose's hands.

"Don't do that. Now that you're here, everything is under control. All the pieces are in their proper position. I am now completely at ease."

"What happened?"

Blade sighed. " Probably any number of my clients are HIV positive or even have AIDS. I've always tried to be careful, but occasionally I get nicked or poked. This is a bloody business. Anyway, I contracted AIDS. I got myself tested when I felt things weren't right. The test came back positive. Of course, there were other tests to confirm the original findings.

"Once the diagnosis was confirmed, I had to make a number of decisions. The primary decision was that I will not wither away until I die. That life would not be worth living. So, I started shutting down the operation. I haven't accepted any new clients for some time and I'm weaning the old ones away. That process is almost complete, with one exception....my dear Rose. You are our greatest creative work....your painting and my needle-work. I had to hang around to complete that masterpiece."

Rose couldn't hold the tears back any longer. She buried her face in Blades hands. The pair sat there until Rose had cried herself out.

Blade withdrew his hands so he could dump the cold coffee and get refills. 'Now I want to see the new painting."

Rose pulled a paper napkin from the holder on that table, wiped her eyes and blew her nose. Slowly she moved to her knapsack to extract the little wooden box. With the same ceremony that Zain had noted when he had viewed the painting, she removed the square of water color paper and placed it in front of Blade.

At first, the tattoo artist leaned back for an overall view.

After a prolonged study, he pulled reading glasses from a shirt pocket and leaned forward to bring the painting into sharp focus.

Rose began to fidget as the inspection continued. Something must be wrong. She had been so pleased with the final panel and now it was being greeted with only silence by the critic that meant the most to her.

Tears were forming again when Blade's eye raised so he could look over the glasses. "Rose, this is truly a masterpiece. And it raises a host of problems."

"Problems, what problems?" said Rose on the edge of panic.

Blade smiled. "All the subtle nuances you've put into this little painting will sorely try my abilities."

"Rubbish, you're the greatest needle man ever."

"American tattooing traditionally makes a big bold statement. Your subtleties would try the hand of the Japanese masters. And this brings up another problem. The panel will ultimately be adjacent to your first panel. The two will be worlds apart. This will be perfectly all right should you wish to demonstrate your various stages of development.

"However, should you want to present a unified image, I'll have to revisit the entire tattoo and add all the little tricks you've learned since we started this project."

"There's that much difference?" said Rose.

"Oh, yes. There is a world of difference. At first, a petal was a petal. Now look at any of these new petals. Each is its own significant little world."

"Can you bring it all together? I don't want part of it to look amateurish."

"Yes. It'll take a while and it will be painful."

"Do you have the time to do this?"

"My dear Rose. Everything else is already set in stone. I will make whatever time is necessary to complete this great work. We'll start tomorrow."

Rose moved into her usual upstairs bedroom. It was comforting to be in a familiar setting. This was her eighth visit. In the last four years she'd seldom slept in the same place two nights in a row. This was the only place where she'd ever completely unpacked her knapsack. Even with the enforced stay at Zain's, she'd still lived out her back pack.

As Rose tried to relax in the age-dated farm house bedroom, she could feel a new tightness in her stomach. Her world was about to change again.

By the time the dinner call came at 6:00, Rose had scraped a sufficient number of self-preservation layers over her feelings so that she could engage in the standard give and take that had developed between the two. Blade was particularly interested in Rose's flood exploits. The tale and all Blade's questions carried them through the evening.

At 9:00 Blade stood up and stretched. "I'm going to make an early night of it. We'll start tomorrow after breakfast."

Left to her own devices, Rose scanned the shelves of Blade's extensive library, but she couldn't find anything that even remotely tickled her fancy. She ended up lying in bed staring into the darkness until the early hours of the morning.

Rose woke to the thumping and bumping sounds coming from the kitchen. She passed through the shower and fetched her short, silk cover-up from the hook in the closet where it had hung for four years. Her flip-flops were still on the floor.

For the next six weeks Rose seldom wore anything but the silk robe. Time was obscured by pain, constant irritation, and with periodic bouts with minor infections. The work was slow because Blade could only work so long before he would get shaky.

After the final panel had been transferred to skin, Blade

started around the tattoo bringing each episode up to the standards set by her final painting. Both were pleased with the results.

Rose shared cooking and household duties with her host so he would not get overtired. Rose came to accept the inevitable. She was able to talk instead of cry.

The tattoo was finished, but a little more healing time was necessary. Over their after-dinner coffee Blade said, “In a couple of days we should be able to do the electrolysis. You know that it may not do a complete job and down the line you may have to touch it up.”

“Yeah, I know.” When Rose decided to have all body hair from the chin down electronically removed, she researched the subject and she was aware of the various problems.

After the hair removal procedure, Blade said, “By Friday you should be ready to reenter the world. It’s time for you to leave.”

Rose remained silent.

“I was waiting to finish your wild roses. Now events are again on the move.”

Although they had never discussed Blade’s plans for himself, Rose knew he was going to kill himself. For lack of anything better to say, she asked, “What are you going to do with the house?”

Blade laughed. “All these years I’ve been able to remain invisible. But, creeping development will soon overtake this place. Deals are being made on adjacent acreages for residential development. Someone will want this forty acres because it lies in the path of progress. The value is in the land. I’m going to have a whoppin’ big fire here to destroy the house, surgery and the recovery rooms.”

“Why burn the house?”

“I can just visualize a new owner getting awakened in the middle of the night by some guy yelling, ‘Come on, Blade, let me in. I’m ready, Cut my balls off.”

Rose had to smile at that image.

"It's set up so my attorney will hold the land until it becomes prime for development. I've got a couple of kids that I know of. The land will pay for their college or set them up in life."

On Friday morning, Rose dressed in her travelling clothes. All her freshly laundered wardrobe was packed in her knapsack. The only change in her appearance from when she arrived almost two months earlier was that she had to gather her ponytail with rubber bands. The little Mexican sombrero had finally crumbled into pieces.

Rose expected that Blade would drive her into town, so she stood by the back door as Blade put the cups from their final morning coffee into the sink. Then he pulled a set of keys from his pocket.

"You'll have to drive yourself. The van is yours. It's in your name, as is the insurance. There are new tires, and my mechanic says it's ready to go. I used it occasionally as a medical transport so there's a cot that folds down from the side. I've thrown in some camping gear and there's some gas money in the ash tray. Go fire it up and head down the road. Don't look back. You're heading into your future. Give me a hug and then scram."

After a long hug, Blade turned her toward the door and patted her on the butt. "Don't let those roses wilt." Blade gently pushed her through the door and closed it behind her.

Rose couldn't talk. Her lower lip trembled and tears blurred her vision, but she squared her shoulders and resolutely set off for the barn where the plain, dark blue Ford van waited in the open doorway.

She parked her knapsack on the passenger's seat. Her seat and the mirrors needed adjusting. As Rose idled by the house, there was no sign of Blade. At the front gate, she turned toward Seattle. Somewhere out there was her future, but she couldn't see where.

In the past, when Rose needed to make a decision as to where to go or which way to turn, she ended up in a bus depot coffee shop. There she could disappear into anonymity as she pondered her possibilities. When her decision was made, she'd step up to the window and buy a ticket to her future.

Eventually, Rose found herself driving around the bus depot. She roused herself out of her muddled thoughts long enough to realize that the bus station was an idiotic notion since she was sitting behind the wheel of a large van.

Rose ended up driving around until she found a Denny's with its own parking.

The lot was sparsely occupied since it was in the post-breakfast and pre-lunch period. Rose parked toward the back. She turned her attention to the van. She needed to know what assets were available to her. The glove compartment yielded the vehicle documentation. The two-year-old van was registered in her name at Blade's address. The insurance papers were there and the premium payment covered the coming year.

The ash tray yielded a fat envelop that held $1000 in twenties. Financially, she was well set. Blade had refused the final payment on her tattoo. It had been a long time since she was so well heeled. At least for the time being, she wouldn't have to look for modeling jobs. However, not working wasn't all that good. Art schools formed a major portion of her social life. She liked the students and faculty. She enjoyed being around creative people

Rose walked around the vehicle and opened the back double-doors. On the left was the fold-down cot that Blade had mentioned. Below it was a line of cabinets that opened toward the center.

Sitting just inside the door was a wooden box painted the same color as the van. It measured about 4x2x1.5 feet.

There were sturdy handles on each end. The top hinged up and was held just past vertical by chains. The front dropped down into a horizontal position. The inner surface was covered with laminate. The series of trays and shelves were filled with cooking and eating utensils. Also there was a full array of condiments. The only thing missing was food.

In one of the cabinets beneath the cot was the food. There was an extensive assortment of canned soups, meats, and veggies. Behind the driver's seat was a water tank.

Rose smiled and shed tears simultaneously as she visualized Blade stocking the van. He was not the camping type but was a thoughtful, loving man, whose caring would carry him where experience failed him.

When she got control of her emotions, she carefully locked the van. Since she was leaving her knapsack inside, she double checked to make sure everything was secure.

Rose headed for the rearmost booth in the restaurant, seating herself facing the corner in case she would start crying again.

For over an hour she dawdled over the coffee, trying to figure out what she would do. Everything was overshadowed by a sense of doom. Blade was going to kill himself. She had been the last loose end. Now she was tied up and Blade would move on.

She tried to envision a scenario where she could prevent his suicide, but Blade had already warned her not to condemn him to an AIDS death. Her only course of action was to wait for what appeared to be the inevitable. She could not contemplate leaving the Seattle area until that was resolved.

Now that she had the van she had to change her modus operandi. She didn't need the shelters now. She needed a campground.

When the waitress came by with the coffee pot, Rose

asked, “Do you know of any campgrounds around here?”

“There’s a bunch of state parks around the sound. In our entry is a Chamber of Commerce display. There may be something there.”

Rose found an area attraction map, which showed several state parks in the vicinity, but there was no indication of which had overnight accommodations.

By the time Rose paid her check, she had a vague, tentative plan of action. She would hang around Seattle until the Blade situation was resolved. She would never be able to live with herself if there was a screw-up and he was only injured and ended up in the hospital alone.

The first three parks were only for day use. Finally, she flagged down a maintenance truck. When asked about camping facilities, the driver said, “There’s Arrowhead about five miles south that has basic facilities. But, if you go another ten miles there’s Totem. It has a full range of facilities....rest rooms, hot showers, wood pile....most anything you need. At this time of year you shouldn’t have any problem getting in. During the season you’d need reservations.”

“Thanks, Totem sounds great.”

Totem was great. It sat on a promontory that jutted out into the sound. She registered her name and vehicle. The attendant said, “There aren’t many people here. Drive around and find a spot you like and come back to give me the number.”

The road wound parallel to the water line with campsites on both sides. At the end of the park the road circled up an incline and returned at a higher level to the entry. Rose selected a spot on the upper tier with a spectacular view over the sound. It was a couple of slots from the rest rooms and showers.

It was only noon when Rose backed into her new home. This was all strange territory for her. She’d never been in a campground before. An inspection of her environs revealed a picnic table with its attendant benches. At one end was a firebox constructed of two, two-foot long concrete strips topped by a cast iron grill. Beside it was a small stack of firewood. There was a sizable open space where tents were probably pitched. Native growth formed a space barrier between neighbors.

Rose locked the van and set out to explore her surroundings. She checked the sanitary facilities. One building contained the rest rooms. On the women's side, toilet stalls lined the walls with four lavatories by the door. The next building had shower stalls on one side and lavatories on the other.

Next to the rest rooms was the wood pile, composed of a great stack of large limbs and tree trunks. The outer fringes of the pile had been cut into smaller chunks with a chain saw.

A white-haired man was attacking the pile with an axe. As Rose watched the operation, the man paused long enough to smile broadly. "A man who cuts his own wood is twice warmed."

Rose smiled back at the old saying. She also couldn't remember seeing an axe when she went through the van. She made a mental note to make sure she had one.

As the afternoon progressed, more campers arrived. Rose continued to wander through the park, picking up tips on how to survive in this artificial wilderness.

Hunger, early darkness and a freshening wind sent Rose back to the van. She would have liked a fire, but she didn't have anything to use as a fire starter. She hadn't found any matches in the van.

Rose certainly didn't want to eat out, so she lifted the camp box out of the van and set it on the end of the picnic table. In the larder she found some cans of food that she could eat cold if necessary.

Further rooting around produced a propane cook stove.

There was even a propane fireplace lighter.

Rose's first evening as a camper found her bundled up in her winter coat, sitting at a picnic bench eating steaming pork and beans and munching on vinegary bean salad. Her vista over Puget Sound was spectacular. The setting sun produced a blaze of color. The salt air tweaked her nose.

It was a pleasant interlude, which evoked images of the one who had made it possible....Blade. The sunset lost its appeal as a knot began to form in her middle.

That same unsettling feeling teamed up with the newness of the sleeping bag, cot and the tremors that ran through the van before the heavy gusting winds to make the night a long one. As the morning light strengthened, Rose headed for the rest room and the paper racks that lined the porch.

The story made the lower part of the front page of the Seattle Post Intelligencer

"A spectacular, wind-whipped fire consumed a farmhouse, stables and barn, killing, the owner Marvin Maloney in his bed. Maloney, who reportedly did contract scientific experimentation, had lived at this location for twenty-five years."

Rose made her way back her campsite while blinking away tears. She moved the stove out of the wind so she could boil water for instant coffee. While the water was heating, she mechanically went through the motions of cleaning up last night's dinner mess. Winter was making its presence felt.

After packing up, she warmed her hands on the coffee cup as the heater pushed back the chill. Her last connection with Seattle no long existed. Just as she had done as the bus pulled into town, she stuffed the past into a mental cubbyhole to be dealt with at some later time.

Rose had no ideas of the shape of the future except for one firm decision....head south until she could shed her winter coat. She hooked up with the coastal highway and turned left. Since she had no time schedule, she wandered from one seaside town to another. She'd never spent any time on the western beaches.

The vast stretches of driftwood fascinated her. Great jumbles of flotsam, cast upon the shores by repeated storms, were trapped in the sand. Rose could spend hours wandering through the debris of decades. Strange shapes tickled her imagination.

At Tillamook, Oregon she was delayed because of a toothache. If it had been anything worse than a simple filling she would have looked up a service organization that provided free dental service for the poor.

While waiting in the dentist's office for him to find time to slide her into his schedule, Rose had a lot of sitting to do. She was methodically going through the magazine offerings even though they were not particularly of interest to her. As she thumbed through a copy of *Architectural Digest,* a floral painting caught her attention. It was hanging on a wall between a kitchen and a breakfast room. It depicted what appeared to be a vast array of wild flowers painted on old, weathered boards that had been covered with white paint.

Something spiked her imagination. All through her dental procedure she wondered if she could paint wild roses on boards and have them come out as appealing as the wild flowers. She'd never worked in anything but watercolors. The wild flowers had been done in opaque paints.

After leaving the dentist's office, Rose backtracked around Tillamook Bay to the town of Garibaldi and the nearby jetty park where there were miles of drift. She pulled up to a log barrier on the far side of a decrepit, old step van. She nearly ran over a pile of driftwood stacked beside it. Rose backed up and swung wider to park. As she changed from sneakers to rubber boots she had purchased to use during her sand exploration, she surveyed the pile of debris next to her. It was a weird assortment of odd shaped and textured pieces. There was part of a wooden box with dovetailed corners. The most colorful item was what appeared to be part of a plywood boat that had three layers of bright paint shining through.

Rose climbed through the driftwood until it was getting late enough that she figured she should be getting a space in the campgrounds. She headed back to her van, dragging two pieces of beach distressed lumber. The edges had been rounded off. Nail holes had been reamed out and much of the soft wood had been abraded away. The distressed surfaces and edges would look great as a background for wild roses if she could figure out how to get everything together.

When she got back to her van, a skinny, raunchy young man was loading the pile of driftwood into the step van.

"Hi ya. If you're looking for lumber there's a whole bunch over against the jetty."

"For the moment, this will probably be enough to find out what I need to know. You've got quite an assortment there."

"The more the better. This is raw material for my sculpture."

"Sculpture?"

"Yeah, I use this stuff to make a sculptural statement. It's amazing what you can say with these bits and pieces. And look at the textures that mother nature provides. See that knot on your wide board? It would take you hours to duplicate that raised grain effect and it wouldn't be half as good."

"Do you sell your sculptures?"

"Sure, that's how I make my living." With a small touch of pride, he said, "I'm a professional."

Through Rose's calculating eye, he must be a low

level professional. Judging from the state of his clothes, personal hygiene, and transportation he hadn't risen too high. However, making a living out of art was a new and interesting concept to her. Rose suspected there was a long tour in the art minor leagues before those that could cut it made the big leagues.

"What'cha going to do with those boards?"

"I'm not quite sure. I saw a picture of a floral painting on boards. I paint wild roses. I'm wondering if I could put them on boards."

"What medium do you use?"

"Watercolor."

"You'll have to switch to either oil or acrylic. Watercolor is too transparent."

"Have you ever painted on wood?"

"Not personally. But, when I was in art school, painter friends played around with it."

"I guess the first thing is to buy a saw to cut these boards."

"I've got a table saw at my studio you can use, if you'll wash the sand off. Sand does bad things to saw blades."

"Where's your studio?"

"Just on the other side of Garibaldi. As soon as I get all my treasures loaded, I'm headed home. You can follow if you like. If you want to cut those boards up, take them to the shower at the end of the parking lot and wash the sand off."

Rose found a stand pipe with a shower head. At this time of year there were no bathers.

When she got back, the sculptor was putting the final pieces in the van. "Toss them in here. That way you won't get the back of your van wet. It doesn't make any difference here. Oh, I'm Alexer."

"Rose."

"Nice to meetcha', Rose. If we get separated, I'll wait for

you at the little bridge on the other end of town. There's a big Garibaldi sign there ."

Rose wasn't all that taken with Alexer, but he seemed to have the information she needed.

They didn't get separated, so Rose was still tagging along behind when Alexer crossed the bridge and signaled for a left turn to take them up the creek away from the highway. A short distance up the road, the van turned across a sagging log bridge. Rose hesitated, but she figured that if that big step van could make it, so could she.

The house was an old, run-down summer cottage with a detached garage to which a lean-to had been added. The materials for the addition were right off the drift piles on the beach.

"This place doesn't look like much, but it serves my purpose and I can afford it. The owner doesn't care what I do. He's keeping it for future development. Some of my sculptures are on the front porch."

He wants to establish his credentials, thought Rose as she fell in behind the skeletal figure as it headed for the veranda porch.

Stacked along the wall were fifteen or so pieces with bases.... ready to sell. Rose's initial impression was much the same as when she'd first gazed across the beach driftwood....an untidy jumble. Alexer detached a piece from the group. It was a part of a creosoted railroad tie. An enormous force had cracked the timber about eighteen inches from the end, putting a sharp kink in the 8x8. On the short end piece was a heavily rusted rail plate, dangling by one oxidized spike. Alexer had sawn the end of the longer portion of the tie at such an angle that when it was mounted on a base, the plate visually balanced the thrust of the lower part.

Rose had sat through hundreds of hours of sculpture, painting and drawing classes listening to dozens of art instructors talking about balance, thrust, asymmetry, texture, visual weight and so forth. She never thought of applying those concepts herself, but she found herself saying, “The warm rust color is spectacular against the cold, dense black of the timber.”

Alexer gaped at her. “Where'd you go to school?”

“I had two years of college, but not in art. I was a business major.”

“You don't talk like a business major.”

“I used to model in art classes. Maybe some of it rubbed off.”

Rose had to gently disengage from the sculpture conversation. “It's getting late. How about seeing your studio before I have to go find a campsite.”

“Oh, yeah, Would you like a cup of coffee or a soda before we saw up your boards?” As Alexer swung the front door open, a blast of fetid air washed across the porch. Rose could see a sink board stacked high with unwashed pots and pans. Dirty clothes littered the floor and were festooned over furniture.

Rose was dying for a cup of coffee, but no way was she going to take on that heavy a bacteria regime. She opted for a soda.

Alexer returned with two generic colas before leading the way to the studio. The deficiencies in housekeeping were not evident in the studio. Everything had its place. There was sawdust around the bench saw, but that was current mess, not like the archeological ruins on the sink board. The studio was loaded with tools....both hand and power.

Alexer was obviously proud of his work space. “I keep an eye on the pawn shops and resale places. I've built a tool inventory for woodworking as good as the school's. I can do metal work except for casting.”

Rose was impressed, so she didn't have to fake her appreciative comments. “This is great. You do all that work in here?”

"On good days I can open the garage doors and pitch my woodcarving chips outside. If it's dirty work, I try to do it in the yard."

"I've been around a lot of painters and draftsmen. They carry their world around in a paint box or pencil box. They don't need such an assortment of tools."

"An artist always needs space....cheap space. You'd be surprised how much space a painter needs. When you stretch your own canvas, you have materials and tools to store. You need somewhere to keep your paintings, and if you do your own framing, that requires even more space. If you're a studio painter, you need even more."

"I'd never thought about that before. I know a bronze sculptor who has tons of space. I figured he spread out so much just because he could."

"What do you want to do with your boards?"

"I'd like to put them together so they look like a painting canvas."

Alexer pulled the two boards out of the van. "One's 1x6 and the other's a 1x8. The standard canvas sizes are 16x20, 18x24, 24x30. You've got enough length so you could make one 16½x24 and one 22½x30. That's pretty close to standard size.

"How'd you come up with those dimensions?"

"A 6" board is really 5 ½" wide and an 8" is actually 7 ½". If you cut three lengths it would be three times the width."

"Oh great, let's do it."

Alexer took over. His table saw had wide wings with measurements marked in both direction from the blade. He set a piece of steel the size of a brick at 24". He put the end of the board against the brick to get the length and moved the wood through the saw. He flipped the board so the other weathered end was against the marker. "Always use the weathered ends. They're much more interesting.

Quickly he cut both boards. From a scrap pile he made four cleats to go across the backs. From a battery of jars whose lids were nailed under a shelf, he selected nails that were just short enough so they didn't penetrate the face.

In virtually no time Alexer had two driftwood panels leaning against a work bench.

"You make it look so easy," said Rose.

"Oh, it is easy if you have the tools. If you plan on doing a lot of these panels, I'd look to getting metal straps to hook them together. The wood cleats are fine, but rather unsightly and they hold the panel too far from the wall.

"They look great. Besides, I'm only going to be experimenting. I've got to get those backgrounds white and I have to buy some paints before I can mess them up."

"Stop by a paint store. They are always making mixing mistakes. They sell those miss-matches for about $3.00 per gallon. There should be a light color you can use. You can coat a hundred of these with a gallon."

"Is there a paint store in Garibaldi?"

"You'd have better luck in Tillamook."

Rose glanced out at the sun, which was dropping toward the ocean. Oh, it's getting late and I haven't found a camp ground yet."

"Just a little ways past where we met is Jetty Park. It has good accommodations."

Rose started to collect her panels.

"How about just leaving them here. Get your paint.... latex, not oil....and come back here. I'm going to be working in the studio all day. Oh yes, get a cheap brush." Alexer held up his hand with about three inches showing between his fingers. "You can paint your panels here. I've got some acrylic paints around here somewhere. I'll dig them out and you can try them. You can probably figure out pretty much which colors you'll need. Acrylics are expensive. There's no sense spending money on something you don't need."

Rose was always on guard. She couldn't detect any malice or danger in Alexer. He was a little strange and very dirty. On the other side, he had a bunch of knowledge and experience she wanted to tap.

She leaned the panels back against the bench. "Gee, thanks. That would really help. This is just a hairbrained idea and I can't afford to spend much on what may be a lost cause."

Alexer was right. It was a nice park. Rose found herself getting excited over the prospect of producing wild roses on panels. She wondered if it was a marketable product....this is if she could do it. The night was one long flood of wild roses trying to align themselves in an artistic arrangement on a panel. In the morning she awoke exhausted and somewhat depressed. She hadn't been able to successfully fill the space. Wild roses didn't have long stems as did wild flowers. Also she didn't have a variety of colors to spread around on the surface. She couldn't enlarge the wild roses because it wouldn't look right.

All through breakfast and the cleanup, Rose's doubts continued to grow. Normally, she was a very positive person, but this project had her by the throat. Never had she had such self-doubts.

Then when she got to the paint department of the builders supply and looked at the sea of weird colors represented by a big dot on the tops of the cans, she returned to the van. She was ready to stick the key in the ignition, start up and continue on to catch the southern sun.

Her state of mind irritated her greatly. She had suffered through hard times such as when her dad died and then her mother. Her whole life plan changed when she couldn't go back to college. She was still working on the Zain thing. Then there was Blade's death. She certainly didn't want Zain to find out what a wimp she was being. It would be difficult enough to let even Alexer glimpse her weakness.

Finally, Rose climbed into the rear of the van for her little painting box. She pulled out one of her tattoo paintings.... not the last one....that one was too valuable to risk loss. Armed with a color sample, she returned to the store.

Eventually, she came up with an off-white in a very pale dusky green. It would make a cool background for the warm pinks. Her hours of sitting on modeling stands were paying off.

With a decent background color in hand, Rose was in a better frame of mind when she drove across the log bridge. The garage doors were open. Her approach had been covered by the persistent sound of a machine. In the middle of the studio was a make-shift table on sawhorses. Her two panels rested on a bed of newspapers.

Rose followed the noise through the back door of the lean-to where Alexer was creating a cloud of sawdust with a grinder as he attacked a large slab of wood. In his peripheral vision, the sculptor caught her motion. The machine went silent and Alexer straightened up, flexed his back as he said, “Good morning.”

“Good morning. What are you making?”

“This is one of my purely commercial projects. When I’m banging around on the beach, I come across all sorts of things. One item I watch out for is burls. When I find a big one, I take it over to a friend who has a jippo sawmill. He cuts the burl into slabs. When I get time I sand them down into coffee table tops. People pay healthy prices for them. This is the fifth one from one burl and I have two more slabs to go.”

Rose, who had been studying Alexer, turned her attention to examining the intricate, interwoven grain patterns. “What a magnificent piece of wood.”

“Wait until I get it down to an 800 grit and slap some varnish on it. Then it is really spectacular. Did you get the paint?”

"Yeah, it's on the table," said Rose as she followed Alexer back into the studio. There had been a subtle change in his appearance since the previous day. His shirt and pants were old and raggedy, but clean. The crud had been knocked off his boots. And his hair was no longer a stringy mess. At the moment it was covered with sawdust, but the dust wasn't sticking in grease.

"That should be a good color," said Alexer as he eyed the smear on the top of the can. He pried up the lid. "You should have had them shake it. He reached under the bench for one of the multi-colored sticks in an old, battered tin bucket. He held up the narrow slat. "I tear apart louvered shutters. They make great swizzle sticks for paint. Take the can outside on the dirt. It has separated. You'll need to mix it thoroughly. Better take that little stool. It'll take a while."

Alexer went back to his sanding as Rose stirred paint. As she switched hands again, she reinforced her memory to have the clerk run the can through the shaker the next time.

When the paint was creamy, Rose carried the can inside. Alexer took the wet stirrer away and set it in a can along the wall to drain and dry.

"Have you ever done any house painting?"

Rose shook her head.

"Well, you want to apply enough paint to cover the surface, but brush it out enough so it doesn't run. Stroke along the grain. Dab the ends of the boards....especially the sawn ends to fill the pores. And finally, keep the paint off the back. A prospective customer would consider you sloppy and not professional if you can't control where you put your paint."

He handed Rose the brush and returned to his sanding.

After some hesitation, Rose dipped the first half inch of her brush into the paint and started her project. A few minutes later, Alexer stuck his head in the door.. Without saying anything, he stepped over to take the brush. He dipped the bristles three-quarters of the way down into the paint, scraped the excess off on the lip of the can and in a few long strokes equaled her laborious production. He handed the brush back and returned to his project.

The next time Alexer came in, Rose was staring at two painted panels and holding a dirty brush like it was a strange, uncouth bug.

"There's a hose by the back door. Clean your brush until no more milk is coming out."

The water was cold and painful on her hands, but she was determined to properly clean her brush. She'd been there less than half an hour and she'd had multiple demonstrations of what a novice she was. Alexer was a fount of information she would like to tap, but at what price? Yesterday, she'd been completely repulsed by his lack of hygiene, both personal and in his habitat. However, today he was clean. Also she was eyeing what looked like a big laundry bag and two stuffed pillow cases sitting beside the back door.

When Rose got back to the studio, Alexer was again on his sander. Sitting on the table next to her panels was a shallow, homemade box that contained a dozen or more little lidded jars.

The machine went silent. Alexer came in dusting himself off. "Those panels will have to dry for at least an hour." He shuffled his feet and looked distinctly uncomfortable.

"I have an apology to make."

"Really, for what?"

"Well, very seldom does anyone ever come here. It wasn't until yesterday that I realized what a slob I have become. After you left last evening, I went out onto the porch to see what you'd seen when I opened the door. I'd seen your expression when I asked if you like some coffee. I wouldn't have accepted that invitation if I'd seen that disaster area. My nose told me even more.

"So I spent a good portion of the night cleaning house. This morning I didn't have any clean clothes to wear. I had to go to the ragbag to get these until I can get to a Laundromat. I think I have the kitchen sanitized sufficiently to again offer you a cup of coffee."

Rose was startled by such a wide-ranging admission. People generally don't lay themselves that bare. "Yes, I'd like some coffee."

This time, when the front door opened, a strong whiff of cleaning materials greeted Rose. That was preferable to stale sweat. Alexer seated her at a small table while he poured two cups from a freshly scrubbed drip pot. The counter top was cleared and clean. The porcelain sink was stained, but those were probably permanent.

When the two were seated at the table, Rose said "Alexer. I've never heard that name before. Is it foreign?"

The owner of the name laughed. "No, nothing that exotic. My name is Alexander. I'd always been called Alex until I moved to another school. Alex was already taken by a girl named Alexandra. Allen already had dibs on Al. To keep everyone straight, the kids added the first two letters of my last name....Ermin....thus Alexer. It stuck and I kind of like it now."

They passed a convivial hour engaging in small talk. Alexer wasn't wearing a watch. Rose had already noticed the absence of any radio, TV or clocks. Despite the lack of timing instruments, at the appropriate time, Alexer said. "It's been an hour. That paint will be soft, but if you don't get too ambitious you should be able to work on it.

"I've got some watercolor brushes in the van."

Alexer shook his head. "Red Sable?"

"Yes."

"Save em. They're too good to waste on experimenting

with acrylics. I have some old acrylic bushes. You can get a feel with them. Are you an easel painter?"

"No, I've always worked on a table."

"Good. My easel is rather rickety."

Alexer gave Rose a crash course in acrylic painting with admonitions on how fast the pigments dry out when exposed to air. "And remember, you can't reconstitute them with a wet brush like watercolor. Once acrylics dry, they are there for an eternity."

By the time Alexer went back to his sanding, he'd just about scared Rose out of even attempting to paint a rose. She made some tentative strokes on the glass pallet, but she couldn't bear messing up those fresh, clean boards.

Finally, Rose went out to the van for the rose panel she'd taken into the paint store. She'd use it as a study just as Blade had done. Periodically, the sander shut down, but Alexer didn't appear. He continued working on his own project.

It seemed like hours later that Alexer came in to trade his grinder for a belt sander. He looked at the blank panels. "Where are your roses?"

"I haven't gotten up the nerve to ruin them yet. I'm still practicing on the glass.

Alexer reached across her and dipped a finger into the burnt umber jar, smeared it on both hands and scooped up some water. He rubbed his hands together and smeared each of them across a panel. "Now they're messed up. Paint."

The sculptor wiped his hands on a cloth before heading for the house leaving a wide-eyed, would-be painter in a state of shock. When Rose could get her mouth closed, she glanced at her watch. It was well past noon.

Quickly she cleaned the brush she was using, closed the jars of paint before also heading for the house.

Alexer was heating coffee when Rose barged into the

house. “Are those three bags on the back porch to go to the Laundromat?”

After a hesitation, he said, “Yes.”

“I have to wash some clothes too. How about you showing me a Laundromat and we’ll get our laundry done. While its drying, I’ll buy lunch....in a place I can afford.”

“You don’t have to do that.”

“I know it, but if you agree, I have the chance to pick your brain, so it is to my benefit. We can take my van.”

“Oh, I don’t think you want to smell up your van with that cargo. We’ll take mine and leave the back door open.”

Alexer filled four washers to Rose’s one, which didn’t put any pressure on the establishment since they were always geared up for the summer tourist trade. The attendant said she’d throw the clothes into dryers, freeing up more time for lunch.

After ordering, Rose said, “I’m sorry I’m such a wimp about this painting thing. For the last four years I’ve been painting wild roses in watercolor, but under a very strict limitation. When you touch watercolor paper you are committed.”

“On those panels, if you don’t like it, you can paint it again with the acrylics or paint out the whole thing with the house paint. Forget the watercolor paper.”

“Also I worked on only one composition. I don’t know how to fill up the space..”

Rose reached into her jacket to pull out the little panel she’d taken into the paint store. When she laid it on the table, it was Alexer’s turn to get round-eyed.

“Wow. This is beautiful. You really know how to paint roses. All you have to do is learn a different medium.”

“There’s something else I’ve got to learn. This is the only composition I’ve ever used.”

Alexer turned the painting 180 degrees. “There is no top or bottom to this. It works both ways. This wasn’t made to hang on a wall."

"No. It was the study for this. Rose rolled over on one hip and raised herself off the bench as she pulled down the waist band on her jeans exposing the top of her tattoo.

"Wow, neat!" exclaimed Alexer in a voice loud enough to attract attention. Rose dropped back onto the bench and Alexer started apologizing profusely for calling attention to themselves.

"You see my problem. I need to learn how to smear paint and do it in a pleasing composition."

"Don't worry about it. All you need is practice. It will come with a little time. If you can put roses like this onto panels you won't have any trouble selling them. In fact, if you can paint in a line like this one, you should be able to do some long panels that can be hung either horizontal or vertical. What a decor item that would be."

"I hope some of your enthusiasm rubs off on me."

"Let's pick up the laundry and get back to the studio so you can paint roses."

The afternoon was a nervous one for Rose. Painting wild roses in acrylics was a real challenge. Despite the cool weather, she wound herself up into a nervous sweat and she reeked. By five o'clock she was a wreck. She needed to get out of there and relax.

Alexer had changed jobs. He was carving a hole in a log so he could glue in a rusty spike. "I can't drive the spike in without knocking off the rust and breaking the attached chain links loose."

"I've got to call it a day," said Rose. "It's getting to me. Can I come back tomorrow to attack it again?"

"Sure, no problem. I'll be here. Or, for that matter, you can camp right here. You know where the water is and you can use the bathroom inside. I'll leave the light on....and close my bedroom door."

Rose didn't even hesitate. "No. I want to be alone to think.

The campground is just what I need right now. Thanks anyway."

After a stop at a market and paying the ten dollar fee, Rose returned to her old camp site. She went through the motions of preparing and eating dinner while pondering the future, which was going to take a lot more work than she had expected. Alexer seemed so enthusiastic about the commercial potential of the panels, the idea must have some merit. However, she still had no handle on what kind of return she might expect. Would it be worth her time and energy? Alexer and Zain made a living out of their art, but their sales items involved a lot more work and expense than a little bit of paint on a piece of driftwood. It would be a lot easier just to plunk down on a modeling stand.

The next morning Rose was in a better frame of mind. She was over much of her negativity of the preceding day.

Alexer had returned his shirt and jeans to the ragbag. He even had a haircut. Also there had been more energy expended in house cleaning.

As they were having coffee before going to the studio, Rose said, "I'm having trouble getting the right pinks. They were all too cold."

"See. You're beginning to find out about your medium. You need different reds. Just a minute."

Alexer disappeared into another part of the house. When he returned he spread a color chart on the table. "Here are all the delicious colors. Alizarin Crimson has too much blue. There are several other reds that make different pinks when tinted."

"Tinted?"

"When white is added. There are probably better greens too."

"Is there an art supply store around?"

"Yeah, but they stock only what would be just minimal displays in real art stores. The best bet is to order from this catalog. The quality is much better and there's a big difference in price....even considering postage.

"I don't have anyplace to send it."

"Send it here. It'll only take a week or so. You're not going anywhere until you conquer acrylics, are you?"

Rose shook her head. "You seem to think I can do it."

"Sure, you already know how to do it. You just have to figure out how to use a new tool."

The next few weeks became a blur of activity. Rose ordered paints. When they arrived she had to learn their new mixing qualities. She filled her panels with roses numerous times and then painted them out.

Alexer made periodic sojourns to the beach. Rose tagged along and gradually built up a supply of panels. She also collected a number of long boards for her elongated compositions.

Rose was amused by Alexer. He was in a production blitz, showing off for his guest. His creativity and productivity were elevated to an all-time high. The porch was getting crowded with a selection of good pieces.

Rose determined to her own satisfaction that Alexer was no particular threat. He didn't appear to have any hidden agenda. When she felt safe, she took him up on his offer of camping next to the studio.

At first it was rather awkward for them to split up to prepare their individual meals. Ultimately, Rose agreed to share the kitchen if she could also share in the cleaning and the kitchen chores. The two of them really sanitized the kitchen and appliances.

Gradually, a routine was established where mutually acceptable breakfast items were stocked. Bread and sandwich making materials were on hand for lunch. Dinner was the chef's choice. They alternated daily.

Early on, Rose made up her mind that she did not want to get into any entangling alliances with Alexer. He was a nice guy but not her type on any prolonged time scale. However, she was beginning to build some doubts in her mind. Here was the third guy in a row who had not made a pass. She could understand Blade with his AIDS, but first Zain and now Alexer. Had she become sexless?

Most of their evenings were spent in the studio doing small jobs and chatting. Rose had eventually showed Alexer the full set of rose panels and he had put two and two together to realize the extent of Rose's tattoo. She knew he was dying to see it, but he was too bashful to ask. However, he wasn't opposed to hinting.

Rose enjoyed the light verbal fencing that went on. She knew that her stay in Garabaldi was only a momentary detour. Soon she'd be moving on.

Alexer was sweet but not of any lingering interest to her. However, that didn't mean she couldn't use him to boost her flagging ego. The day had been spent on the beach collecting. She'd gotten dirty and sweaty. After dinner, Rose turned her chair sideways to the table and began unlacing her new beach-boots. She announced that she needed a shower. She removed her boots and socks and stood them along the wall. As she began to unbutton her heavy wool shirt, she smiled sweetly at Alexer, who was as motionless as a mannequin except for his eyes.

Rose shrugged out of her shirt and hung it on the back of the chair, leaving her in a white T-shirt. Alexer was scarcely breathing. Hooking her finger in the bottom, she stripped it over her head. She wasn't wearing a bra.

Alexer wasn't at risk of suffocating, because when her shirt came off there was a heavy gasp. He got another lung full when she unbuttoned and unzipped her jeans. Hooking her thumbs in the waistband, she slowly lowered her pants and panties as she gently gyrated her hips. Alexer breathed again when the roses appeared.

It wasn't until Rose stepped out of her jeans that Alexer

had anything to say and then he repeated himself. "Wow." And kept repeating himself as she did a slow undulating rotation.

"After a long day at the beach, don't you need a shower too?" cooed Rose.

"Yeah," came a vague reply followed by a more assertive, "Sure." Alexer bent over to remove his boots. Rose ran her fingers through his now clean and shorter hair.

Alexer's hands suddenly became populated with thumbs. As he struggled with his boot laces, Rose was of no help. She kept up a rhythmic dance so that her tattoo undulated inches from his eyes. Once the footgear impediment was removed, Rose guided Alexer into a standing position while she tugged his shirt and T-shirt over this head leaving it entangled on his arms. While Alexer was making final disposition of the shirts, Rose opened his fly and had his already alert member in hand. It conformed to its owner, long and skinny. Rose had to jerk herself back to the moment as she found herself comparing Alexer with Zain.

The pair made their way to the tiny, tin shower stall where they both started giggling as they tried mutual washing in the stingy confines. Eventually, they ended up on Alexer's cot, which was no more commodious than the shower. It had a metal frame which folded in half for easy transport. The cot had a thin pad for a mattress. Both were going to exhibit bruised elbows and knees the next day.

Although Rose had guarded against over-exciting her partner in the shower, she was still going to have await a revival before concluding the evening.

As Rose gathered her clothes to go to her cot in the van, she wore a contented smile. It had been a fulfilling encounter and it had done wonders for her ego. Although her partner lacked experience, he compensated with enthusiasm.

The only hitch in the evening had come when they were relaxing after their final encounter when Alexer said, "I suppose this means you're leaving."

Caught by surprise by that assessment of her actions, there was a moment's hesitation before she said, "Yes, eventually I'll be leaving, but I hadn't planned on doing so yet. This was not payment for anything, only a desire for an intimate interlude for mutual enjoyment. I owe you a lot for all you've taught me and your consideration, but I don't pay my bill with sexual favors."

Day by day, Rose was becoming more competent and more confident with her painting. With the new colors, she could get the nuances she wanted. She became adept at handling opaque pigments. Her new virtuosity was further advanced when an order of new brushes arrived.

A looming problem was the number of panels she was accumulating. Initially she painted and repainted the two original fabrications. Eventually, she produced something she wanted to keep, which meant new panels had to be made.

Rose had to face up to another concern. She was getting too comfortable in what she knew could only be a temporary situation. Alexer was a nice kid, but he was not her type. She needed the challenge of an alpha male.

One morning Alexer said, "You've been worried about pricing your work. Put a couple of your paintings in the van. I've got to make a gallery run. We can ask the gallery people how they would price your work if they were to handle it. I'll be going to two galleries....one in Lake Oswego and another in Portland."

"How many galleries do you have?"

"Only two inland. My stuff seems to sell better, but at a lower price, on the coast. People get fascinated by driftwood while they're on the beach."

"How do galleries work? I only know about student and faculty galleries in the schools where I modeled."

"You have to take examples of your work into a gallery.

They decide if your work is good enough, if you fit into their philosophy and whether or not you conflict with anyone else in their stable. If you're accepted, they'll tell you how many pieces they want to inventory. That depends on the size of the gallery, storage and other factors they think are important. A contract is signed. Contracts vary widely. Most galleries want exclusive representation in a given area. You and the gallery establish a price and the gallery gives you half when the piece is sold."

"Half?"

"Yeah, half. Some of them are trying to go up to sixty percent."

"That's awfully expensive wall space."

"Right, but you get exposed to their client list. I know one gallery that does ninety-five per cent of their business on six nights a year. That's when they stage major shows. They must stay open the rest of the year for that remaining five per cent."

"Is that one of your galleries?"

"No. I'm not a big enough name to make it there. They specialize in large works of well known artists."

At the Lake Oswego gallery Alexer introduced Rose to the proprietor. More as a favor to Alexer than as an accommodation to Rose, he agreed to look at the paintings and give his thoughts on pricing.

Rose brought in one panel and a single board on which she'd painted a background stripe leaving a lot of the board natural. She'd painted an elongated edition of her tattoo study.

"Oh," said the gallery owner. "These are nice. They aren't what I expected. Just a moment. Let me call my associate. She deals more in this form than I."

When the owner reappeared he was accompanied by a gray-haired lady who exuded elegance and grace. "This is Elizabeth. She is well attuned to the local market. Of course, you know that prices can vary widely from one area to another."

Without waiting for an answer, the owner headed for his office leaving Elizabeth to make the assessment. She didn't remain long before excusing herself and joining the owner in his office.

"Are they that bad?" said Rose.

"I don't know what's going on. Elizabeth really knows her stuff. She'll be back."

Alexer was right. Elizabeth came striding back to Rose. "We think the panel would bring eleven hundred dollars. Although the long painting has fewer flowers on it, it is unique enough to command twelve hundred dollars."

Rose didn't show any outward reaction, but she was astounded. She had secretly hoped they would bring her a hundred....maybe a hundred and a half. Her only points of reference were the various student and faculty galleries she wandered through while posing in the art schools.

"If you are interested," continued Elizabeth, "we would be willing to handle these two for you, since I have an idea where I can place them."

Rose nodded. "That would be great."

"Come back to my office and we'll complete the paperwork."

Alexer stepped aside. "I'll bring in my new pieces while you ladies finish up."

As Elizabeth was filling out the forms, she said, "Did Alexer explain that we charge 50% of the sale price?"

"Yes, that's fine. However, let me explain something. I'm really a transient. For some weeks I've been parking my camper at Alexer's while he's helping me with my painting. This was an unexpected layover and soon I'll be moving on. I have no idea where I will land. I have no permanent address.

"I owe Alexer a great deal for all the help he has been.

He's a sweet guy. If these paintings sell, please send Alexer the proceeds. But, don't tell him about this arrangement ahead of time."

"That can be done. I'll draw up an agreement to that effect. Are you going to be able to supply the gallery with additional paintings?"

"I have no idea," said Rose. "I've just lost my anchor, so I'm adrift. When I beach myself, you'll be one of the first to know."

Elizabeth finished drawing up the contracts. While Rose read them over and signed them, Elizabeth went out to deal with Alexer.

On the way out of Portland, Alexer detoured off the highway, ending up in a parking lot of a pawn shop. "Let me show you how to buy tools."

Rose trailed along as Alexer cut through the electronics and household appliances to the tool section. Rose's first impression was that she was looking at a junk yard of old, battered, rusty chunks of metal. Alexer obviously had another point of reference. He ooed and awed over dirty pieces as he minutely inspected each piece. He made his way to the circular saws. There were a dozen lined up on the shelf. Several were obviously rejected out of hand. His attention settled on three, which apparently rated closer inspection. The field was quickly reduced to the Milwaukee.

"This is a good machine. It is a quality brand and easy to find repair parts. The blade is sharp and the saw hasn't been abused."

Alexer marched over to the counter and got involved in a deep discussion with the clerk. Eventually, Alexer paid eighteen dollars instead of twenty-five.

On the way back to the van, Alexer handed Rose the saw. "This is a going away present. You're going to have to cut those boards."

As Rose took the machine, she said, "Oh, Alexer, what a wonderful, thoughtful gift. You've already been so helpful.... and patient. You didn't need to buy this. How can I ever repay your kindness?"

"This has been a mutually beneficial period. One thing is that you jerked me back from slobsville. And you probably haven't noted any difference, but I've been looking at my own work with a much more critical eye."

"What do you mean?"

"You approach your wild roses looking for perfection in every petal, leaf, thorn. I got to looking at my work. It was sloppy. The joints between two elements were strong enough, but they didn't join perfectly. There are a whole bunch of things, I'm doing differently since you came into my life. Many things have changed."

Suddenly Rose was apprehensive of where Alexer was going. She fervently hoped he wasn't going to make a passionate plea for her to stay and proclaim his everlasting devotion. She didn't want to hurt him, but she had other ridges to crest.

Rose was relieved when Alexer acknowledged her impending departure with, "When you're gone, I have to evaluate my life. Right now, my little found object sculptures are a meal ticket. They provide me with walk-about money, but nothing for the future."

"I know what you mean," said Rose. "I need to look to the future too. It's going to get here quicker than we think."

Back at the studio Rose started collecting her things. She was appalled at the sheer volume of her painted panels and boards. She could get them into the van, but there was little room for anything else. She would have to remove some to get to her cot.

Alexer listened to Rose grouse about space. Finally, he said, "You can delay your departure one more day, can't you?"

"Well. Yes. There is no firm date."

"Remember me telling you about all the lumber down by the jetty?"

"Sure, it was too new for my likes."

"But it would make a nice carrier to go on top of the van."

Rose had never paid any attention to the chrome railing that ran around the roof. She only used the ladder on the back door as a drying rack for her undies.

They picked up enough lumber from the beach to construct a big, flat box that could handle more panels than Rose had on hand. Alexer sloped the front so as to be more aerodynamic. He took pains to see that it was watertight. The crowning touch came when he attached one of Rose's long wild rose boards to each side.

"I'd suggest putting some varnish over the roses to help preserve them."

That night after dinner, Rose and Alexer got together for the last time. They had learned to drag the mattress pad off the springs to prevent bruising their ankles, knees and elbows. It was a relaxed, pleasureful interlude for them both.

In the morning, Rose joined Alexer for coffee and breakfast. Both were subdued. Parting would not be easy because a mutual fondness had developed. When the time came, they walked out to the van together. Rose got in and started the engine. She stuck her hand out the open window and they held each other for a moment, while Alexer again reminded her to send him a address as soon as she had one.

As Rose negotiated the turn in the road that would obscure the studio, she could see in the rear view mirror that Alexer hadn't moved.

At the Coastal Highway, Rose pointed the van south, still intent on outrunning the cold.

CHAPTER 13

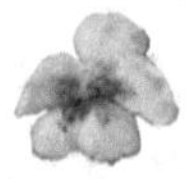

Zain was pleased with the Greco-Roman wrestling book that the boys brought from the school library. It was well illustrated with excellent photographs of starting position, take-downs, moves and counter-moves.

With Erik on one side and Emil on the other, Zain sat at his drafting table, thumbing through the book. Then he flipped back to the front.

"Guys, this is the drill for the next few weeks. I want you to select one of these positions. Once you've decided on the right one, I'll take a series of photos of you two in that position. Then you are to use those studies to sculpt a joint piece. If you do a good enough job, Judge Winters might be inclined to buy a copy. If he wants one, then we'll cast it for him when we get to pouring metal."

"You mean 'buy' our sculpture?" said Erik in wonder.

"Right, but he has to like it. Just because you make a sculpture doesn't mean he'll like it enough to buy it."

"How much will he pay?" asked Emil.

"That's not important now," said Zain. "The important thing is making a sale. That means that someone likes your work well enough to take his hard earned cash out of his pocket and put it in yours. When you're starting out, you have to earn your way up the ladder."

"How big is it supposed to be?" said Erik.

"That's what you have to figure out once you decide which pose you're going to use."

Zain left the boys pouring over the book as he did some busywork around the studio. A big altercation broke out on who should have the advantage. Neither wanted to be depicted in the lesser position. Zain let the controversy rage. He retired to his computer.

The following day the boys announced their decision. It was a photo of the beginning of a take-down where the opponent was countering. Neither wrestler had an advantage at the moment.

Emil explained their choice. "You always say it's good to show action. Most of the starting positions make them look like they have roots in the ground. In this one, they are moving, but neither has a point yet."

"Good thinking. Now if we use a 13 inch tile as a top to the base, how big should the figures be?"

Zain led the boys through all the various considerations. When the decision was made, he sent them out to weld up their armatures.

Zain was getting close to calling Arty to help him make molds. It was becoming a chore keeping all his clay pieces at proper humidity. Winter had arrived. Zain kept his studio heated. He also humidified the air to keep his sinuses and sculpture from drying out.

This was the largest project Zain had ever attempted. Doing the sculpture had been the joyful, creative part of the operation. Now he was faced with months of just plain, hard dirty-work. He was becoming somewhat depressed at the enormity of the tasks ahead.

Zain decided not to sculpt any more pieces. He had enough to mount a major show. If he had his druthers, he'd continue sculpting until he had a long, white beard instead going on to the next step.

CHAPTER 14

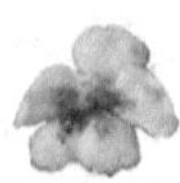

On Sunday afternoon, Erik and Emil were in the studio deeply engrossed in their sculpting. Zain gave them a brief critique and let them return to their work. He was feeling slightly jealous that he didn't have his hands in clay, too.

As he plodded back to the house, he heard a car trying to negotiate his snow-covered driveway. It turned out to be Judge Winters. His family wasn't with him on this occasion. A tall, dignified man stepped out into the snow.

"Zain, I'd like you to meet a friend, Haley Mallette. Haley was one of my professors in Law School. We've kept in touch through the years. I'd like to show him my latest acquisition and, for that matter, he'd like to see what you've been doing."

"Pleased to meet you," said Zain as the two men shook hands. "Come into the studio. My apprentices are in there working on their dual piece."

When Zain opened the studio door, he knew the boys had peeked to see who was there. They'd thrown cloths over their pieces when they saw the judge.

Zain introduced the two boys before asking them to get out number three. As they moved to comply, Zain picked the cloths off their sculptures and pinched a hunk of clay off the foot on Emil's piece.

A plaintive wail came from the other side of the studio. "I told you that foot was too big."

Mallette was shown the judge's piece, as well as a representative sample of the others in the series. Zain also had the boys display their work.

As the boys started replacing the works, Mallette said, "Ray tells me you make a wicked chicory coffee. Do you still have any of it around?"

It surprised Zain that his guest would invite himself in for coffee. "Sure, it'll only take a bit to make a fresh pot."

Ray and Mallette settled down at the kitchen table while Zain stoked the coffee maker. "I neglected to mention," said Ray, "that Haley is also the owner of HM Gallery....the most prestigious gallery in Denver."

Zain acknowledged the information with a nod of the head, but his pulse rate took a jump. To maintain his cool demeanor, he busied himself with the coffee service, although he was pretty sure no condiments would be necessary. He would let his guest start any conversation about the gallery.

It was Ray who opened the discussion. "I've been telling Haley about your work for some time. He wouldn't take my word for it. He had to come see for himself."

"Oh, I believed you, but how could I pass up a chance to get out of town? Zain, I like your work very much. And if you can cast all these pieces, you'll have a nice show. Of course, there's a lot of work and money necessary before any commitment can be made. I understand you will be doing your own casting. We will want to see the finished product."

Zain had been leaning against the drain board waiting for the coffee to make. "Naturally. I'm not ready to commit to anything at this early stage. But I certainly appreciate any positive feedback I can get. Thank you."

"Have you set a completion date?"

"In theory, I should be able to finish up in a year, but I also know that is an unrealistic expectation. There are too many hiccups along the way. I can shoot for it, but a better working date would be the following spring. Of course, everything is predicated on money and luck that nothing disastrous happens."

Zain poured the coffee. His guests seemed content to remain in the warm kitchen. The rest of the house was pretty chilly.

Mallette was full of questions about Zain. He was particularly interested in the original girl and towel concept.

"A good show should embody a good story. Two, if you can get them," said Mallette.

Zain smiled....and he didn't even know about the tattoo.

"What are you going to do with the boys' sculpture?"

"I'll cast them along with the rest. I want them to go through the whole experience. They've really come a long way. A few months ago they hadn't yet made the connection between the painting and the painter, let alone a sculpture and a sculptor."

"I think," said Mallette, "that another of the good stories would be to show your apprentices' work. There is a little room right off the main gallery that could handle their work very nicely."

Zain laughed. "What an experience that would be for a couple of fifteen-year-olds....tending their own show."

"I'll bet I could get Pam to chaperone them," said Ray, "She thinks they are absolutely darling."

"Don't let them hear that they are 'darling'. I'd never get them out from under the barn."

Ray continued. "I'm impressed with that new piece of theirs. When I was thinking of a dual piece, I had something entirely different in mind, but this concept is much better. Was it your idea?"

"Not really. The Greco-Roman wrestling was, but the pose is entirely theirs. In fact they gave me a lecture about getting implied action in a piece. And that was hard to do when neither wanted to be in the inferior position."

"I'll probably take number one of that piece, but don't tell them yet. Say that I want to see the wax before making my decision."

As his guests left, Zain saw two eyes peering out of a crack in the studio door. They were pushing the dinner time limit, so he went out to relieve their anguish.

"The judge likes your work so far. He wants to see it when both figures are together. I told him he could look at the wax when it was ready."

Both Erik and Emil wiggled like happy puppies. Zain wondered what their reaction would be to being offered to show in the major Denver gallery. That would come later.

Chapter 15

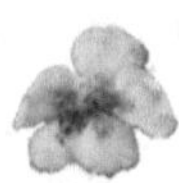

The possibility of a major Denver show sparked new enthusiasm and energy. However, Zain ran into a roadblock when he called Arty Gossnell, the mold maker, and found that he would not be available for at least two weeks due to a family emergency.

Zain extracted a promise that Arty would come as soon as possible. This change in his production schedule left him strangely at odds with the world. A silent conflict that had been going on for some time surfaced....Rose. He had been letting his work prevent his scratching an ever more irritating mental itch. That damn kiss threw all his rationalizations into a cocked hat.

Now that he had some time, he was going to have to try to find that odd female to see if he'd blown an opportunity. Since the holiday travel rush was over, it would be less of a hassle to get to Seattle.

After the dinner hour, Zain trudged along the path the kids kept clear to the Vasa house. The family was still in the big country kitchen cleaning up the dinner mess. Zain accepted a cup of coffee and a chair from Emil....after a frown and a head motion from Carina reminding her son of his social obligation.

"I can't get the mold man here for at least two weeks. And that's the next step. So, I've decided to take a few days off."

Zain looked around the table. Carina was smiling knowingly. The older girls started to giggle. Even the corners of Bo's mouth curled up. Erik and Emil both had big smiles.

"What?" said Zain. "I'm just going to see the Rodin show in Houston."

All the smiling faces fell.

"Okay. I'm really going to Seattle." His announcement brought a cheer even from the little kids, who had just figured out what was happening.

"Inga, will you feed Wolf and Nutsy?" Looking at Erik and Emil, he said, "Please keep the sculptures in good shape. I'll be gone a week or two. I really don't have a schedule. There's too much snow and cold for my old van, so I'll fly.

The trip was uneventful. Zain picked up as cheap a rental car as he could. He located a reasonable motel in an older commercial district. He was always mindful of how much bronze he could buy with every ten dollars he could save on his expenses.

His first exercise was to go through the phone book listings for hairdressers, looking for the name "Blade." Finding nothing he passed on to tattoo parlors. Still nothing. He also made up a list of art schools in the area. He'd come fortified with a portrait of Rose and another showing the tattoo as he last saw it with the blank panel.

The next morning Zain spent on the phone calling hairdressers asking if they knew a guy names "Blade." No one could provide him with any information.

Next he started making the rounds of the tattoo parlors. No one recognized the name "Blade." None of the tattoo shops could identify the artist who worked on Rose. When they found that the roses had been designed by the recipient, they said that the tattoo artist probably suppressed his own individuality for the sake of the painting. That was why they couldn't identify the tattoo artist.

Four days into his investigation, he hadn't gleaned one iota of useable information. His only remaining line of inquiry was the art schools. Although Rose had mentioned that she had never really frequented the local schools, Zain couldn't afford to pass up any possible source of information.

However, he immediately found that locating the ones that might have any information was going to be a problem. The life drawing instructors wouldn't be in until the next day. The life sculpture instructor's class was at night. It was a whole day of frustrations. He even tried to get the schools' disbursement officers to see if they had paid "Rose." School policy blocked most financial inquiries.

The next morning, he headed for the closest chain drugstore to use their digital photo equipment. He scanned the back shot of Rose and her tattoo. Then he cropped out out a section of roses with enough anatomy showing to leave no doubt as to geography. From that view he made a stack of prints.

As he made the rounds of the art schools, he left an envelope for each of the instructors who used nude models. It contained a photo and a message asking for assistance in locating Rose.

Zain wanted to allay as much as possible the perception that he was just an old letch chasing a girl, so he gave the school where he taught as the contact address. He also put in his email address and the motel phone number.

That evening he got his first nibble. A message had been left while he was at dinner.

"Hi, my name is Zain Zook. You called a little earlier in response to my call for assistance.

"Yeah, I'm Ron Elder. I teach life drawing at Seattle

Commercial Art. I used Rose as a model a couple of times. She was a great model."

"I know. She was just perfect for a series of sculpture I had in mind. How long ago did she work for you?"

"The first time was probably three years ago. Then she passed through town again about a year ago and came wandering into my class. At the time, I was using a perfectly horrid model. Was I glad to see her."

"Then you haven't seen her for a year or so?"

"Right, but I was talking with a friend who teaches in San Francisco. He knows Rose. Apparently, she has a route. From Seattle she heads south. I know she gets as far south as LA because my friend recommended her to an associate of his who has a program in LA."

"That's good to know. She came to Seattle after she left Colorado. Maybe I can pick up her trail. Do you by chance know her full name or where she came from?"

"Rose is all I know. She always avoided giving out any personal information. I suspected she was avoiding a bad husband, but that may just be a figment of my imagination."

Zain received two more calls which provided less information than the first. He was left with decisions. When someone says they are going to Seattle, that doesn't necessarily mean just the city. There were a myriad of smaller communities huddled on the outskirts of the city. Rose could just as well have been headed for one of them. He didn't have time to investigate all of them.

Probably, she was no longer in the area. He didn't know how long it would take to get the new tattoo applied, but it should have been finished months ago. The chances seemed good that she had moved south.

It appeared that Rose had a regular trap line. Zain called Ron Elder.

After some small talk, Zain said "Say, Ron, could I get

the name of your friend in San Francisco. If Rose hasn't passed through yet, I could leave a message with him. And I might be able to find her in between."

Later that evening, he made contact with San Francisco. Rose hadn't shown up. Zain left word for her to call him in Colorado.

Next he booked a flight to Portland, Oregon where he used the phone to make the rounds. One of the instructors at Portland State had used Rose's service for the last three years. She hadn't necessarily shown up at the same time of year, but because she was such a good model, he always made room for her.

Zain left a message at two Portland locations before he caught a flight back to Denver.

Chapter 16

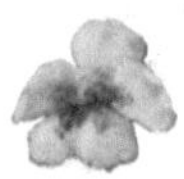

It was late afternoon before Zain slithered up his snow-clogged driveway. The keening cry had gone out before he could get out of his van. The thundering herd was already pounding up the hill.

"Did you find her?" came calls from at least four sources. His negative answer keyed eight prolonged and disappointed "awes."

Erik and Emil had already grabbed his flight bag and suitcase. Wolf came bounding from wherever he'd been sleeping. Nutsy was seated in the kitchen window.

Zain was glad to be home. He was particularly relieved to be able to shed the gloomy speculation that had occupied his thoughts during the trip home, that Rose was fleeing a bad husband or some other trouble. It was indeed good to be home.

The whole entourage shuffled through eight inches of new snow to the back door. Since the boys had his luggage, Zain walked between them with his hands on their shoulders.

"How's the 'duet' coming?" Duet was the name that had been attached to the joint piece the boys were doing.

"We put it together," said Erik. "We think it's done until you pinch off all the clay."

"I only take off things that shouldn't be there. If you didn't put them there I wouldn't pinch them off."

As soon as the gang got into the house, Inga started feeding the animals. If there was an animal involved, Inga wasn't far away.

Finally, little Kas was able to get a word into the excited conversation. "Mom says you're supposed to come down for dinner."

"Okay. That's only twenty minutes from now. You guys clear out and do your chores. I'll get cleaned up and come down."

Zain checked the mail on the table....just junk and bills. One of the messages on his answering machine was from the mold maker. Zain was to pick him up on Saturday.

Not too early Saturday, thought Zain. Arty would be counting on being fed and boozed over the weekend. Oh, well, that's a small price to pay for that caliber of work. Arty was a happy drunk. He would get a silly grin on his face and settle down until the only coordination he had left was exhausted just getting his hulk into bed, where he slept like the dead. In the morning, he'd shake off the effects of all that beer by his second cup of coffee. He was then ready to put in a full day of competent work.

To be on the safe side, Zain would talk with Bo and Carina after dinner so they could help keep the kids away during Arty's indisposition.

Dinner was a grilling match on what he did to find Rose. The kids were relentless and Carina gave them free reign. She wanted to know too.

Bo just sat back and listened until at the very end he asked the hardest question of them all...."What next?"

Zain didn't have an answer for that question. "I don't know. The only thing I know now that I didn't know before

I left was that she apparently had an itinerary or route from Seattle south and it would appear she has broken that pattern. I can't go running all over the country without more specific information than I have now."

"Maybe she'll get one of your messages and call," said Elen hopefully.

"If she's not modeling anymore, she won't go to the schools will she?" asked Emil.

"In any case," said Zain, "the only thing I can do is to call some people and have them give me a shout if they hear anything."

"Who can you call?" said Carina.

"Oh, I know a few teaching artists. I can also call some of the obvious schools, such as the Chicago Art Institute, Students Art League, and major art schools. Rose mentioned a few of them while she was here."

At 11:00 AM Saturday Zain pulled up in front of a low rent apartment house. Arty was waiting on the stoop. Zain suspected Arty didn't want his living conditions put under scrutiny. Arty tossed his travel bag into the back, shook hands and settled down in front of the heater.

No mold making got done, but Zain was able to delay the first beer until after Arty had inspected all the sculptures and the piles of materials that had been accumulated.

"You're going to be short on plaster."

"How much?'

"Half a dozen bags at least."

"How about shims?"

"You're all right unless we ruin too many. If we have to, we can cut up some beer cans. Do you have a good supply?" Arty laughed at his own joke.

Zain came back with, "Oh, we have enough. I kept the excess cans from when you were here before."

Arty shook his head. "No, it's got to be fresh metal. All those old cans would have hardened by now."

Once the inventory was inspected, Zain led the way to the refrigerator. He picked up a beer for each of them before establishing Arty in the pink room. Even though Arty had stayed there before, he bounced on the bed, ran through the channels on the TV that Zain had installed and checked out his side of the bathroom. When Arty plopped down on the bed and took a long swig of beer, Zain knew that his mold-maker had settled in for the duration.

Monday morning, work began in earnest. Zain had the feeling he had to go at double time to keep up with Arty. It wasn't that Arty worked so fast....it was that he worked so efficiently.

Mold-making was a very precise craft. A soft, fragile clay figure had to be encased in a rigid plaster shell that could be taken apart without damaging the soft figure inside. Later, that casing would be reassembled so that hot wax could be poured in and permitted to form a thin layer in the mold before the residue was poured out leaving a hollow wax positive of the original clay piece. When the wax hardened, the mold would carefully be removed from the wax and then made ready to pour another edition if required. Otherwise, the mold would be reassembled to prevent distortion and put into storage until it was needed again.

In the sizes that Zain was working, there was a lot of heavy lifting. Also it was a dirty process.

By the time Erik and Emil got in from school, Zain was ready for a break, although he would have died before letting Arty know that he'd driven a man half his age into the ground. There'd been a brief noon break for soup and sandwiches....not beer.

Normally, Arty didn't teach. If one could learn by watching the master work, that was fine. That was how Zain had become a competent mold-maker, even though he hated the process.

Zain had asked Arty if he would explain the process to

the boys as he went along. Zain had expected his request would be ignored. However, when the boys blew in the door like an excited eight-legged puppy, Arty growled at them. "Sit." He pointed at two stools he'd placed earlier, just out of the range of plaster splatters.

"There isn't any room for error in this business unless you want the sculptor to ram an oversized, serrated clay loop up your ass. Now shut up. Exercise your ear....not your lips."

The boys squirmed on their stools, glanced at Zain before turning their undivided attention back to Arty after they got a very serious nod from Zain.

Arty started giving a running commentary on each of his actions. As the work and the blow-by-blow description continued, even Zain listened intently. The dissertation not only described the work at hand, but how the process developed historically and technologically. It continued for an hour and a half until the boys had to go to dinner.

That signaled quitting time to Arty. He marched into the kitchen, got a beer in each hand and headed for his room to await dinner. When Arty came down for more beer, Zain was just pulling a tray of lasagna from the oven, so Arty went to his place at the table to wait for dinner to be served.

Zain said, "Thanks for giving the boys all that information this afternoon."

"That's the first time I've ever done that. I like their sculpture. How much of it is yours?"

"The only time I touch their pieces is when I pinch off something that doesn't work. They have to do it again. I guess you can say there's a lot of me in their work because they've never seen any other sculpture. Oh, their eyes have passed over sculpture, but they didn't see it. They use me as a model on how it should look."

"Figured as much. They've got some talent. Maybe with a

poke in the right spot, they'll amount to something."

"I told you about my possible Denver show. If that comes off, the gallery will probably offer Erik and Emil a little show of their own in a side room. They don't know about this yet, because the powers-to-be want to see their finished work before making the offer.

"The boys should help on their own pieces. Save their work until they're around." That was the end of the conversation until Arty sopped up the last of the olive oil from his salad bowl and popped the final piece of Italian garlic bread into his mouth.

"You'd better show them about undercutting. They may want to revisit some of their pieces," said Arty, as he picked up his comments where he had left off.

Zain let Erik and Emil watch a couple more days before he had them go back into their pieces and eliminate any undercuts that would have kept the molds from releasing cleanly. By that time they had a good understanding of what had to be taken into consideration when a rigid mold was to be used. After that, both boys were covered with slopped plaster and dust. Zain had insisted they change into grubbies before working with Arty. He didn't want to add to Carina's already humongous laundry load. They also found out that mold-making was hard work.

Arty wouldn't work on weekends, but he would socialize with what was now a pretty constant flow of visitors. Hawk spotted a story in Arty and his mold-making talents. And a little vignette would be a continuation of the popular earlier feature on Zain. The studio was becoming a wonderful artistic backdrop for feature filming. Besides the number of draped sculptures, there were now racks of drying molds. They had to be kept under heat in a Colorado winter so they wouldn't freeze and crack.

Then there was also Erik and Emil. Hawk had gotten good mileage out of the pair in the past and there was certainly more to be garnered. The problem became timing. Hawk couldn't convince Arty to set up a demonstration on the weekend and the two boys arrived home too late for him to shoot the story and get back to the station for the evening news.

Zain had to give Hawk credit. He stuck with his story. Eventually, Hawk got everyone to agree with a plan where he would pick up the boys at school in the studio helicopter. He even got an hour cut off of their school day. Then Arty was going to work on a mold of the dual sculpture with the boys assisting. After a brief interview, Zain would go into the background to remove the clay from a new mold. Arty and the boys would become the central characters.

Fortunately, Hawk had inadvertently broadcast a warning not to bother the studio during the week by telling of all the dispensations he had to get to be able to film his report within the normal work period. Arty stayed for three weeks. Zain was glad to see him go for more than one reason. He now had the house back to himself. He didn't have to cook for a house guest. And above all, the molds were made. The next phase of the operation was to pull the waxes. The boys were ambivalent about getting their piece to that stage because the judge had said he'd make a decision at that time as to whether he would buy or not.

It was nice to dream about their first sale, but it would be devastating if he said "No." Some days they thought their piece was great and at other times they knew it was lousy. They would end up asking Zain what he thought of the dual piece. Zain always gave a non-committal answer that satisfied neither....so the anguish continued.

Zain didn't have enough wax to pour more than a few pieces. Microcrystalline wax was very expensive in the quantities he needed. During the burnout, where the wax was melted out of the investments, forming the cavities into which the molten bronze was poured, a certain amount of wax could be recovered. However, he was still going to have to buy a lot more.

Besides the wax, there was the refractory material for the investments and then the bronze.....and a lot of propane. Zain was beginning to worry about finances for his project. Everything was a bit more expensive than he had estimated. Also, he had executed more and larger pieces than he had originally envisioned. And he had the boys' pieces to consider.

Zain spent many nights at his computer running figures on projected outgo and possible income. He was sitting on a chunk of wealth, but his inheritance had a bunch of restrictions and one of the most important was that no encumbrances should be placed on the property except under certain circumstances. An art show didn't fall under "certain circumstances."

The only route that seemed open to Zain was to forge ahead as far and as fast as his supply of materials and available money would take him.

Out of his limited supply of wax, he made it a point to pour the small piece the judge had bought. As soon as he could get it translated into metal, the rest of the purchase price would be due. He also worked on the two large pieces that had attracted the judge. Of course, if the judge bought the dual piece, the boys would get more money than they had ever had in hand in their young lives. They could pay for their own casting.

Once the first batch of waxes was complete, Zain called Judge Winters telling him that the dual piece was ready to view. On Sunday, the Winters sedan pulled into the yard. Erik and Emil had been warned that the judge might drop by, so they came dragging their feet up the hill.

Zain engaged in some small talk with the Winters until the boys arrived. He then led the way into the studio. The boys were petrified. Zain had placed the dual wax on a textured, green slate tile. That in turn was atop a three foot display stand, centered under the model lights. The bronze colored wax gave the allusion of metal.

Pam grabbed Jeffy as he headed for trouble. She shoved the toddler's hand into Erik's saying, "Hold onto him or this will be a disaster area before you can bat your eyes." Turning to Emil, she thrust Molly into his arms. "I think you know how to handle one of these long enough for me to see, too."

Pam joined her husband walking around the piece, making critical comments. The boys were too busy with their wiggling charges to get overwrought by hearing random comments about their work.

After the inspection, Pam retrieved her two offspring, leaving the boys to deal with the judge.

"Have you set a price on this piece?" said the judge in a very business like manner.

Both boys looked at each other with wide eyes and shrugged. Of course, they had talked about prices, but they had no basis to make a judgment. They knew the purchase prices of Zain's work, but he was a professional grown-up.

"I'll tell you what....I'll give you half the price of Zain's piece."

The boys gasped.

Zain said, "Even though they can't seem to say anything, I'm sure they'll agree to that. It is a more than generous offer."

"It's a remarkable piece for a couple of young lads. The story behind it makes it worthwhile."

"I told you it was all right to be both handsome and talented," said Pam. That started the blushing, which got even deeper when she added, "And with physiques like those...." Pam added a throaty growl.

"Oh, Pam," said Ray. "Leave the poor boys alone. Let

them enjoy their first sale." Turning to the boys, he said, "I'll expect each of you to sign your own sculpture and give the piece a good name."

The judge pulled his checkbook from his jacket pocket and wrote a $500 check to the order of Erik Vasa and Emil Vasa. "You'll probably have to have your dad with you to deal with this money. Congratulations on a fine piece of sculpture. Now you boys go show this to your family while I talk some business with Zain.

Zain had started the coffee when the Winters car drove into the yard. Everything else was ready, so they just paused in the kitchen long enough for Zain to put the pot on the tray before heading for the library. While Pam was looking for some more French reading, Ray said, "I also want one of eight on your 'Victory' piece if it's available."

"The wax that is in the studio is my artist's proof, which I plan to keep. One is available."

"Good." The judge pull out his checkbook again to write the down payment check. "How's the show coming?"

"It's just a matter of time and money. This will help a lot," said Zain as he waved the judge's check. "But, I'm going to have to raise a lot more money. Because of the TV coverage, the gallery sold a couple of pieces. It all helps. This property is all tied up in the estate restrictions. It's my only asset."

"I'm not so sure. Have you ever sat down and figured the value of just this show when you consider there can be at least eight of each piece offered for sale? That's considering you keep the AP on each. Once you come up with the sum, try to think of any other business in the county that is manufacturing a product that comes anywhere close to you in a like amount of time. You are a known entity with a proven track record. You have or will have considerable assets.

"When you get into that realm of worth there are probably

several sources of financial backing available to you.

"I know a VP at one of the local banks who has a little, gentleman's ranch up past me. Convert your terms from those of an artist into those of a businessman and he might entertain a financial deal."

It was Zain's turn to look dumb. This was a whole different world. He'd have to turn in his art magazines for the Wall Street Journal to learn the nomenclature of business.

After an extended hesitation, Zain said, "Artists usually make lousy businessmen. That is not a subject taught in art school."

"You don't have to have an MBA to apply for a loan. Without any qualms you could go to the bank to take out a mortgage on this place, if you could. All you have to do is change a half-dozen words and the bankers will do all the rest."

As the Winters family drove down the hill, Zain came to the conclusion it had been a very propitious Sunday. The boys had made an unheard-of sale for a couple of fifteen-year olds. He had a sizeable check in his hand along with one of the judge's business cards with the banker's name on the back and his mind was still spinning from the persuasive pep-talk the judge had given concerning his chances of financing the rest of the show.

His thoughts were interrupted by Kas yelling at him from down the hill that he had been invited to a party.

When Zain arrived at Vasa house, he was carrying a sheet wax about a foot square and a handful of little tools, which he gave to Erik and Emil. "Now it's time to develop your signatures. You need to sign your sculptures. Decide on what name you want to use and how you want it to look. I've seen many a nice piece ruined with a lousy signature. Be professional."

CHAPTER 17

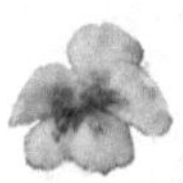

Zain had figured the money needed to mount his show and it scared him. He was beset with all sorts of trepidations when he went for his appointment with the banker. The financial man minutely went over his figures and decided that Zain had been entirely too conservative. "It would certainly be unwise to run out of money before the project was complete. You'll need at least twice this amount."

Ultimately, Zain had a line of credit on which he could draw, as needed.

Zain had to pull another wax for the piece the judge had purchased. The first wax was to be the artist's proof, which he set aside because he was going to give it some special attention.

At first, Zain looked to Erik and Emil for help moving the plaster molds once they had cured and lost their excess water. When more muscle was needed to work the foundry, he looked to the school where he still taught the Monday life class. Zain posted a notice on the bulletin board that he needed bodies for a certain stage of the process. He usually had a surplus, which worked out all right. The extra people ran the pizzas through the oven and kept the sodas coming. Zain didn't permit any alcohol or drugs in his studio.

Spring turned into summer. One after another of the waxes turned into bronzes, which were set aside for later chasing of sprue marks and flashings. Any pits or bubbles would have to be welded.

Periodically, Zain phoned the various art schools around the country looking for Rose. He switched to email for economic reasons and because he could send messages at night instead of spending his daylight hours on hold on the telephone

Finally, arrangements were made with the gallery. Originally, the show was set for the late fall, but one of the gallery's exhibiting artists had a fire that damaged a lot of work, so Zain was moved up to the spring. That shortened Zain's preparation time.

The banker had been right. Zain had severely underestimated his expenses, but because of the generous credit line, Zain had the money to have a professional foundry put on the patinas.

Zain rented a large truck to haul the pieces to the Zellwood Foundry. While the sculptures were gone, Zain and his apprentices worked on bases, a process Zain hated almost as much as mold-making. But a piece is not ready for sale until it is finished.

It seemed to Zain that he had been on this project half of his adult life. Erik and Emil were no longer little kids. They had found girls. And they could spit just as well as baseball players. Zain was grateful that they had maintained their intense interest in sculpture.

Inga and Inger were blossoming into attractive young women with developing chests. Zain had lived through the piano scales and now the sounds coming from the music room were tolerable. The girls were getting particularly adept at four-handed pieces.

The girls' main line of interest could best be described as animal husbandry. Inga was into breeding everything in sight. The farm yard was taking on the attributes of a zoo. All sorts of strange creatures clucked, hissed, whistled, chirped, brayed, mooed, or whinnied through the daylight hours. Bo turned the farm's livestock breeding program over to Inga. However, it was Inger who nourished and nursed the menagerie, because once the critters were hatched or born, Inga lost interest.

Little Kas and Ken were not so little any more. Kas had always had trouble getting a word into a conversation. One day the boys watched a mime on TV. From that day on, the twins began building their own repertoire of mime moves, which developed into a private language for themselves and a source of entertainment for others. They were building their own reputation at school.

Elen and Elsa were still concentrating on becoming big people with all the rights and privileges of their older siblings.

Finally, the show date was on the top page of the calendar. Zain bought a new midnight blue suit, blue tie, light blue shirt and black shoes. A large truck was reserved and the motel reservations were made.

Zain was financing the opening trip. The boys would ride with him in the truck. The Vasas would follow in their van. When it came to accommodations for the Vasa family, he couldn't find a dormitory so he settled for connecting motel rooms.

As the date approached, Zain's thoughts turned more and more to Rose. He expanded his search of the art schools and phoned those where he had made contacts months before. No one had seen or heard anything about Rose, leaving him to conclude that she'd either settled down with her hairdresser or she'd reconciled her differences with whomever she was fleeing. His conclusion left him with a distinct feeling of loss.

Zain had to have the show there a day before the opening, which meant the entire entourage had to come at that same time because Zain had the boys with him. The rest of the Vasa family was not involved in the setup so they were free to shop and sightsee in the big city. Zain included Erik and Emil in the entire pre-show process. They got back to the motel just in time to clean up and dress before the opening. The twins donned new slacks, sport shirts, and shoes. Pam had wanted the gym shorts.

The opening itself was a blur of constant activity. The crowd was large and noisy. The show was one of those Denver events where people went to see and be seen. And martinis were served. Zain was not good with names and he retained very few of those who were introduced to him. He was able to avoid the perils of the martinis by carrying around a glass of water with an olive in it.

Pam was shepherding the boys and having a perfectly delightful time. Bo and Carina, with the kids in tow, made an unobtrusive appearance. Zain took a moment to watch two obviously very proud parents revel in their first-borns' glory. The other twins were in utter awe of the event and their brothers' part in the whole affair.

Finally, the lights blinked and the crowds drifted away. As the adrenaline seeped away, the exhibitors and the gallery personnel were ready to crash. Zain's primary thought was that finally the ordeal was over. The show would stand for a month, but his labors were pretty much complete and he could now turn his attention to new projects.

CHAPTER 18

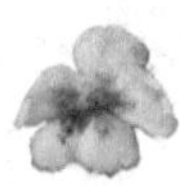

As Zain drove along the road to his house, he noted a big RV parked next to the Vasa house. He knew there were other branches of the family scattered around the northern states. From the size of that barn on wheels, the propensity for twins must extend into other parts of the gene pool.

Zain pulled up to the studio door. He had decided it was time to replace his clay supply. The old stuff had too many plaster bits and other impurities to do any detail work. Before he unloaded the new bricks of clay from the van, he'd clean out the clay safe. It was dirty work, so Zain stripped off his go-to-town T-shirt and shorts before crawling into the large wooden box to scrape the interior with a broad putty knife.

A slight sound and the model lights coming on made him pop up to find out what was happening.

On the model stand stood a naked Rose doing a slow, rotating bump and grind showing off her completed tattoo. After a moment of utter disbelief, Zain vaulted out of the box to rush to his model. He jumped onto the stand where the pair fell into a mutual embrace, to the cheer of the whole pack of Vasa kids who were squeezing through the door.

"Rose, is it really you?" cried Zain, who immediately felt embarrassed for spouting such an inane question.

"I hear you were looking for me."

"Yeah," said Zain as he shut off further conversation with a prolonged kiss. The kiss evolved into as much more passionate expression of his feeling. He was getting a gratifying response.

The pair sank to their knees. Rose continued her hip gyrations, which was causing Zain to stretch his skimpy, navy blue briefs.

Exploring hands moved over both bodies. Zain found the tattoo. "Oh, it's cool," he said.

"This isn't," said Rose as she stripped down his shorts. Never disengaging, but by degrees they slumped down to a horizontal position.

He's going to mount her," came an excited whisper from the direction of the door.

"Shouldn't we take precautions?" murmured Zain.

"Pill," breathed Rose in his ear.

"No Brer Fox, not the briar patch." said Zain as he entered.

"They're going to breed," came another muted exclamation from the corner.

Rose disengaged her lips and one arm long enough to point toward the door and say, "Scat."

There was a general exit while Zain and Rose peeled away layers of frustration that had built up over all those years.

Following a prolonged acrobatic engagement, the two participants remained entwined until their breathing returned to normal. Rose looked over Zain's shoulder and snickered.

"Take a look at that."

Zain rolled over just in time to glimpse eight faces lined

up on the ground on the other side of the van just before they scattered.

"Let's take a shower."

"Can I shower on the green side?"

"I wouldn't hear of it any other way."

Zain and Rose walked arm-in-arm, naked across the yard. Rose paused momentarily to greet Wolf and Nutsy. Their mutual attentiveness persisted through the shower. They finally vacated when the water turned cold.

Eventually, they ended up sitting cross-legged on Zain's bed. Rose wrapped a towel round her damp hair. "The kids tell me you tried to find me."

"After you left, I....I....I missed you." There was a long pause and Rose offered no help. "I don't know how to put this....Oh, nuts, I didn't know if I missed you or I missed the opportunity to get to know you. I don't think that makes much sense. I had the feeling you might be the one I been hoping would come into my life, but I was too stiff-necked to find out and suddenly you were gone."

"I thought you didn't like me."

Zain's eyebrows went up. "What did I do to make you think that?"

"Oh, you didn't do anything. That was the problem. Most guys spend their waking hours trying to get me into bed. For days we shared the same bed....naked....and I couldn't get a rise out of you."

"Oh," said Zain, rolling his eyes skyward. "You don't know how hard it was for me to be a good boy. I always make it a point, out of professional etiquette, not to make a pass at my models."

"I found that out after I left. I asked Devon if you were gay."

"Really, what did he say?"

Rose laughed. "He assured me you weren't."

"When I tried to find you, I didn't even know your

name."

"Abigail Adams."

"From?'

"Kansas. Knowing my name wouldn't have helped. No one knows it."

"Are you married?"

"No. What gave you the impression that I was married?"

"Someone suggested you were running from a brutal husband."

"Nooooo."

"Then there seemed to be the possibility you settled down with your hairdresser."

"Hairdresser?"

"Yes, Blade."

Rose broke out in laughter. "Blade, a hairdresser. Hardly."

"You said he was a cutter," declared Zain defensively.

"Cutter, has another meaning. How should I say it? He was an unlicensed surgeon who did work standard medical practitioners refused to do. I was there only long enough for him to finish the tattoo. Then he kicked me out and committed suicide that night. He was dying of AIDS and that was his solution. It's still hard to think about it."

Rose changed subjects. "What was that crack about Brer Fox?"

"Oh, did I say that out loud?"

"I'm not psychic."

"Well, at first I wasn't taken with your tattoo."

"I noticed."

"After you left, I got to fantasizing about what I hadn't done while you were here. I worried about getting by those rose thorns. Gradually the tattoo wasn't so frightening and every time it came to mind, it brought up the Brer Rabbit fables where he outfoxes the fox by feigning fear of the briar patch so the dumb fox casts him into it."

"Not to worry," chuckled Rose. "No thorns." She rolled back to show Zain he wouldn't become impaled in a crucial area. "I thought of that image too."

A slight sound wafted into the bedroom. "We're about to be up to our ears in kids," said Zain.

"Let'um come."

"Come on in," shouted Zain.

There was a general shuffle, followed by a screaming Viking charge.

Zain flinched as eight more bodies tried to find room on his bed. The frame held. The tattoo and Rose's complete lack of body hair was the initial topic of interest.

As the subject waned, Inga cried above the general hubbub. "Rose, you should see the boys' new circumcisions."

"Oh, how did you talk your dad into that?"

Inger launched herself into the story. "Dad found a retired urologist who was looking for a pot bellied pig for his granddaughter. Inga's Matilda just had piglets, so dad traded one for four circumcisions. The doctor did them on the kitchen table."

"That's not all," said Inga. "Mom was talking to the doctor and ended up trading pairs of P-fowl, muscovies and Australian geese for a circumcision and vasectomy for dad. Now mom's got a safe plaything."

"Yeah," said Inger, "she's having fun with it. She doesn't want any more twins." That brought a laugh from everyone.

"Did he show it to you?" asked Eric.

"Show me what?" said Rose rather guardedly, as she took into consideration the current topic of conversation.

Erik jumped off the bed, darted across the room to throw a wall switch. The dark corner of the room, where Zain had his office, was suddenly bathed in light. The flood lights were directed at the bronze of Rose and the towel in "Victory" pose. However, this edition was considerably different than those he was selling. He had created an exact likeness of Rose in great detail. And the rose tattoo was minutely reproduced in bas relief.

Rose caught her breath and moved off the bed to get a closer look. The kids became unnaturally silent while the model inspected the artist's creation. The only sound was Wolf scratching himself. After a minute inspection, where Rose had not uttered a word, she returned to the bed, her cheeks wet with tears. Kas and Elen moved aside so she had a clear path to Zain. Rose launched herself into his arms as she muttered between kisses, "It's beautiful, it's beautiful."

With self-righteous certainty Erik said, "I told you, she'd like it."

Kas reached across the entangled mass in the middle of the bed to tap Rose on the shoulder. When he had her attention, Kas started one of his pantomime routines. Rose had to pause to interpret. Zain, who was more experienced, translated, "He says, we've been invited to dinner and it's about time."

"Oh," said Rose. "If you'd use the fork in your right hand, more people in Colorado would understand."

"He's been watching that Frenchman," said Elsa

"If we're going to make it to dinner, someone better go get our clothes," said Rose, who delayed long enough to plant another kiss on Zain.

Emil and Inger scurried out to gather the discarded garments. The rest of the kids headed for home to tell their parents of the wondrous happenings.

By the time Zain and Rose got down to the Vasa house, the kids were loudly proclaiming that they were starving. Carina welcomed Zain before turning her attention to serving the meal. Rose backed Bo into the corner so he couldn't avoid telling her what had happened around the Vasa house since she'd left. She'd already heard the kids' stories. Now she want the adult version. Bo being of few words, concisely hit the high points before the dinner call.

As usual, there was little conversation at the first of the meal, but as the appetites were satiated, a clamor arose for Rose to tell what had happened in her world.

She gave an abridged report of going to see her tattoo artist in Seattle and getting the tattoo finished. Generally, she made it sound as if she'd visited the tattoo parlor and the guy had finished the job. Then she said a friend had given her a van. While on the Oregon coast she'd gotten the idea of painting wild roses on driftwood. With the help of a driftwood sculptor, she'd learned the process. Then she'd headed south trying to get warm.

"At first I cut the driftwood into lengths to make panels, but as I went along I found that the long, narrow pieces with chains of wild roses painted on them really fired people's imaginations. At one park, I was painting on a board, and before I knew it, I'd attracted a crowd. A woman asked how much I wanted for it. I had no idea how much to ask when selling one myself, so I said I hadn't thought about price since I was painting it to go on the soffit above the sink. Then I asked her how much she'd give me for it. When her husband said five hundred bucks, I said that soffit could remain bare for a while longer."

"Did he have five hundred in cash?" asked Zain.

"Oh, boy, handling money can be a real pain."

"Tell me about it," said Zain. "A lot of art is sold to out-of-towners. I've taken several bum checks and once some stolen travelers checks."

"This time the wife chased her husband to the ATM while she watched me finish the painting."

"How do you sign your paintings?" asked Erik. "Zain made Emil and me spend hours working on our signature."

Rose looked at Zain, who said, "Oh, that's a story for later."

To Zain she said, "I'll hold you to that." To Emil and Erik she said, "Go out to 'Big Shack'. On the seat behind the table are a couple of painted boards. Will you get them for me?"

"Big Shack?"

"Yes, the RV. That's what I call her whenever I have to refer to that monstrosity."

The boys hesitated.

"Oh, run along. I won't tell any more of my tale until you get back."

They wouldn't have missed much in any case, since the twins were back so quickly carrying a couple of six-foot, 1x8s. Rose directed that one be stood against the wall while the other was laid on the floor against the wall.

Erik stooped down to read Abigail Rose Adams

"Awe," said the whole Vasa family in appreciation of the paintings.

"And no one better call me Abby," said Rose with a stern look as she surveyed the assembled folks.

"Go on with your story," pleaded Elsa.

"I moved my way south toward the sunshine. I was learning a lot about painting and business. I got down to Point Reyes, north of San Francisco. That was a good selling area. For a while I moved up and down the coast in the same general area.

Several problems arose. One was space. I ran out of it. The sculptor up north made a carrier for the rack on top of the van. I soon filled it with driftwood. I needed that to keep painting. I was accumulating too many finished paintings. I was crowding myself out of house and home.

"What did you do?" asked Elen.

"Eventually, I had to buy an enclosed trailer. Then I had to learn how to back up....repair tail lights....that kind of stuff.

"Another problem was that I had too many painted panels.

When I was painting on the beach, the hot item was the long format.

"As I moved up and down the coast I was always seeing signs to Petaluma. It always seemed to be about the same distance away. So I went to Petaluma to set up a bank account so I could take checks. That's when I started signing my full name.

"In Petaluma, I also found a gallery in a sort of mall inside an old building. They were delighted with my panels. I didn't show them the strips until they were just about out of the big ones."

"Sounds like you had a hot item going," said Zain.

"Oh, it took a while. You can't believe some of the stupid things I did along the line."

"I can imagine that. All artists go through the same growing pains."

"I had another problem you never had. As soon as school was out and there were more young males along the beaches, I practically had to beat them off with a stick. When I was painting on the beach....when it was warm enough....I wore short shorts and a halter top. It attracted customers and a horde of horny males."

"That wasn't the tan line I saw," said Zain. His statement was backed up by eight nodding heads.

"That's a later story." Rose wasn't to be distracted. "I didn't want to become a fixture around that area, so I stocked the gallery and moved south. I didn't hang around San Francisco. It was too cold and foggy. Some places were better than others. I'd heard Laguna Beach was a wonderful art community. There are galleries all over the place. However, I was viewed as an interloper. If I wanted to show in a gallery, I couldn't sell on my own unless I paid the gallery just as much as if they had sold it."

Rose thumbed her nose. "You can guess how welcome I was around there.

"I'd been stocking up to be able to supply galleries. I had that van stuffed so full, I had to load the driving compartment to be able to crawl into the cot. Finally, It got so bad I rigged a tarp and slept on the ground.

"One day I was in a beach campground. I got to talking to an elderly couple who were in the next slot. There was a minus tide and the lady was lamenting the fact that neither of them dared to go out on the flats to dig clams because of their arthritis. I really felt sorry for them. The next morning I dug out the entrenching tool Blade had put in the van. A couple of blisters later, I had a half a bucket of steamers. I left the bucket on the steps of their RV."

"What are steamers?" said Ken.

"They are little clams that are steamed open and eaten right out of the shell."

"Ugh," said Kas with a wrinkled nose.

"Don't knock it until you try it," said Rose. "They're delicious. Every minus tide I filled up. Anyway, when I came back from painting, the lady was pouring the shells on the roadway that is made of shell.

"That evening they invited me in for coffee and cake. They were so appreciative of the clams. They had been making the coastal journey every year for two-plus decades, but this was their last trip. It was getting too hard on them physically. They were going to sell their old RV."

Erik made pointing motions toward "Big Shack."

"Yes, you guessed it. As the conversation progressed, a trade became obvious, but I was going to have to pay a substantial difference. I'd been sending checks and extra money to Petaluma, but I intentionally never kept a running balance. I knew the account was building rapidly. When I called to get a current balance, I was sure they had mistaken me for the head of industry. I had enough money transferred to take care of the deal, insurance, license fees, and taxes. California is an expensive place to buy a car.

"We spent a whole day moving stuff. I wish I'd had you kids along to help. The old couple were too feeble to do much. I left all the camping things because they still wanted to have the capability to make short trips. They took all their personal things out, but left the entire kitchen with pots and pan and condiments. They left bedding and bath towels and such. They spent the last night in the RV before taking the van and trailer back home near Kingman, Arizona."

Zain was finding something very humorous.

"And what's wrong with you?" demanded Rose.

"I just have a hard time imagining the travel-light, hitch-hiking liberal girl driving down major highways in a gas-guzzling behemoth like that."

"Yeah, look at me. I entered your world and look what its done. I'm a mess of responsibilities. I have insurance premiums to pay, licenses to keep current and the horror of horrors....I have to pay taxes....both state and federal."

"Welcome to the real world," said Zain with a moderating grin.

Rose stuck her tongue out at him before continuing. "When I tried to move that big chunk of junk down the road, I really questioned my sanity. I gave up painting for the better part of a week, trying to learn how to manage that beast. I ended up back in the LA area.

"At Muscle Beach I made a valuable contact. This towering hunk of a man stopped to look at my paintings. He'd been on the beach some time building muscles, but he finally realized there was no future for him in the muscle parade. He'd lost his job and couldn't find another. He was going to have to leave. I hired him to sit in his little bikini near me while I painted. If someone got too aggressive I'd call 'Dear.' With him around and in areas where it was permitted, I wore a thong and a minimal bra. That really brought in the business."

"I'll bet," said Zain, who didn't look too pleased.

Rose laughed. "Don't get macho on me. Gabe was as gay as one can be. He was in love with himself. When Gabe was running shotgun, I could sell two or three paintings a day. When I could do that, I didn't mind paying him $100 a day to keep the wolves away. I picked him up on the street corner every morning before heading for the beach.

"Well, that's pretty much what has been happening to me." Rose got up to refill her coffee cup and any others that had run down. "What's been happening around here?"

"Erik and Emil had their first sculpture show," said Carina with a mother's pride. "Go get your pictures." Emil tore upstairs for the scrapbook.

"Your own sculpture show?" said Rose with raised eyebrows.

"Well, it was part of Zain's big show," explained Erik.

"What big show?" Rose looked accusingly at Zain. "You didn't say anything about a big show."

"We didn't exactly have time to talk about shows."

Rose ducked her head a bit and her ears got a red tinge. Emil saved the day by thumping the boys' prized portfolio down in front of her. The first page held the half-sheet cover of the slick brochure from the HM Gallery. It featured a photograph of "Victory," the piece Rose had seen in Zain's room, except that this was the generic version. Page two held the inside cover, which had a group picture of Zain, bracketed by the twins. It had been taken in the studio with Zain in his usual T-shirt and shorts, but the boys only had their tiny, gray gym shorts. The three were hefting one of the large molds. The bios were below.

Rose smirked. "Don't any of you guys make any cracks about me showing skin to sell my art."

The inside page and the top half of the back cover were photos of other "Rose" sculptures. The bottom half of the back had a large photo of Erik and Emil standing behind a cluster of their sculptures. This time they were dressed.

Rose didn't take the time to read the numerous clippings from various newspapers and events calendars.

"Oh, my, you guys hit the big time—big time," said Rose in obvious appreciation. Both boys were standing on either side of her as she looked at the scrapbook. She put an arm around each waist and gave them a big hug.

"You didn't ask how we sold," said Erik.

"If you wouldn't think I'm being crass," said Rose in a sophisticated manner. Then she dropped into a conspiratorial theatrical whisper, "How'd you sell?"

"They sold all of them," yelled Elen from the other end of the table.

"Yeah, and they have orders for three more," added Elsa.

They sat at the table for hours catching up on each other's lives. Finally, Carina chased the younger ones off to get ready for bed and the other kids were told to clean up the dinner mess. Rose said she wanted to move Big Shack up the hill.

Carina wouldn't let Rose leave without a grand tour of the house so she could see what the family had done since the flood. Zain excused himself so he could do some of his own sorting and cleaning.

CHAPTER 19

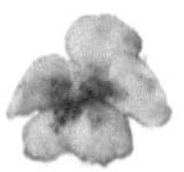

When Big Shack pulled up to the back door, Zain met Rose with a hug. “How about showing me your rolling palace?”

“That can wait until daylight. I want to hear about this big show you neglected to mention. From the brochure, it appears you used some of my poses.”

“Well, yes. In fact you were the whole show....except for the boys' work.”

“Have you a scrapbook as the kids do?

“No, but I have a full portfolio on the computer.”

“Clippings?”

“I've got some, but they're still stored in a box.”

Zain was leading the way toward a freestanding sideboard in the older part of the kitchen. When he opened the door, they were presented with a vast array of booze.

“Wow, is this something new?”

“I seem to have gotten on the local tourist trail. I have people popping in all weekend. I can't complain too much because some have turned into customers. Now I can start boozing them up when we start discussing a purchase. What can I serve you?”

"I'm not too much of a drinker, although there is one I enjoy....a fuzzy navel."

"I think I can handle that."

Zain built Rose's drink and poured himself a brandy before leading the way to the computer. He called up the portfolio and turned the machine over to Rose and retired to his easy chair. Zain had scanned the show brochure into his digital portfolio. That was followed by pages of photos of the pieces. Each piece was shown from the four sides and then the best oblique view. Any thumbnail could be enlarged to fill the screen.

As Rose moved through the display, she made small vocal sounds and rendered tiny hand or body motions, but offered no comments.

Zain, who had been apprehensive on how Rose might take such exposure, was beginning to fidget. He was perfectly within his right since he had all the necessary releases and he'd been straight-forward about his intentions. But, the lack of comment was becoming a major source of worry.

When Rose came to end of the show portfolio, there was another portfolio showing the processes involved in producing the show.

Rose left the computer to sit in Zain's lap. "The Vasas said it was a great show. Now that I've seen it, I concur. My question is, how did the public take it?"

Zain, who hated to toot his own horn, shrugged before saying, "No complaints from me."

Rose looked exasperated. She reach down and with the knuckles of her hand gathered a chunk of skin on Zain's rib cage. She pinched down and twisted.

"Aaaaah!"

Releasing the pressure, but not the skin, Rose said, "One of these days you'll learn not to give me one of your cutesy answers. Now let me ask again. How did the public take it?"

When Zain hesitated, Rose took up the slack in the skin.

"Hey," said Zain. "It's not an easy question to answer."

"Take your time," said Rose as she snuggled down in his lap.

"Well, things started out rather slowly. Because of Judge Winters and his associates, there was as a huge turnout, but no sales. Then the biggest bank in Denver bought #2 of Victory. That must have been the stamp of approval needed to have nudes in collections. Suddenly, corporate plastic was being flashed all around the room. When the business community got through, there wasn't much left. The gallery director explained to the subsequent public viewers that they could buy other copies of the same edition. I've been kept busy filling orders."

"Now, that's a decent answer." Zain was rewarded with a kiss. When Zain moved to continue the intimacy, Rose said, "Not so fast. I still have questions. How did the boys do?"

"The gallery likes stories. Our story started with you back in the flood. You, being the mysterious model that disappeared. All those video tapes taken by Hunter Hawk became part of the story. Many people had seen the TV coverage. The bundle of gym shorts was a major player, since Erik and Emil were shown several times in them. Those two scallywags became the heartthrobs of the junior high school. Then they produced some fine pieces of sculpture.

"All these stories were circulated before the show opened, creating an interest. The stories brought the people in. The boys had a sellout and they still have a couple of orders to fill."

"I love that story and it was all because you took the time to show them how to do it."

"I gave them an opportunity, but it was their curiosity

and drive that made it all come about. They are strong reflections of Bo and Carina."

"What are the plans now?"

"I still have orders to fill. Somewhere along the line I have to find time to paint this joint before the snow flies. Then I have to build an inventory. Those Rose pieces are in demand. My Colorado galleries have their noses out of joint because I gave an exclusive to MH Gallery for the Rosies.

Zain got pinched again. "I never did like Rosie."

"Okay, Roses."

Rose relented and let the conversation lapse into more intimate activities.

Chapter 20

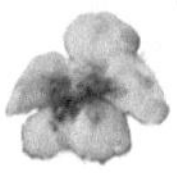

Inga's roosters had long since concluded their wake-up duties and turned their attention to the barnyard hens. Erik and Emil were impatiently lurking around the studio performing unnecessary tasks. Inga and Inger were sitting on the porch steps as if waiting to get to the piano. The two younger sets would have been there too if Carina hadn't impressed them into service at the grocery store. All the twins wanted to be around Zain and Rose. That was where great things happened.

Although the artists had spent a long time in bed, they weren't rested. Rose had to trek out to Big Shack to get fresh clothes and her personal hygienic items. That was the opening the kids needed. They flooded the kitchen to say good morning and ask inconsequential questions.

Zain had foreseen the invasion. Mugs were lined up on the counter. All the kids drank coffee if there was enough milk in it. Wolf and Nutsy were also underfoot. Zain had to move breakfast into the family breakfast room to seat the horde.

After the kids had their visit, Zain assigned the boys studio work. He suggested the girls do their practicing early so Rose could hear how they had improved.

The first item of business was for Rose to show Zain Big Shack.

"I had to do a lot of relocating," said Rose as they stepped in the side door.

"I'll bet the former owners wouldn't recognize this thing," said Zain with a laugh. Snuggled against the dining table was a table saw with its blade retracted. The result was a long working space. The paint smears on the table indicated it had another purpose than dining, despite the salt and pepper shakers.

Rose shrugged. "I needed working space. That's why I bought it. I couldn't paint in the van, so when the weather was lousy I just twiddled my thumbs."

"From the looks of all of this work, you haven't been twiddling anything."

"You haven't seen anything yet." Rose led the way back to the bedroom. Every space was jammed with painted boards or boards to be painted. The kitchen was full of painting supplies. The spice rack on the wall was filled with jars of acrylic paint.

When they got back to the front, Zain plopped down sideways on the passenger seat. "It looks as if you've developed a whale of an enterprise. I'll bet it beats modeling in financial returns."

"That it does." Rose crawled into the driver's seat.

Zain cocked his head to one side and looked directly into Rose's eyes. "Why did you come back?"

It was Rose's turn to fidget. "Actually, there are several reasons." Rose hesitated.

"Start with reason number one."

"I wanted to see if anything was wrong with me."

"What?"

Rose snapped around to glare at Zain. "When I found out that you weren't gay and you still ignored me, then there must be something wrong with me. I knew you didn't approve of my tattoo, but was that enough to cancel me out? Was it something I said or did, or what?"

"Oh," said Zain. A touch of disappointment showed.

The intonation was caught by Rose, who immediately regrouped. "Then I thought you might have been viewing me as a dumb broad with a reasonably good body, who models.

"It was you who got me to thinking that art was something that could be done to make a living. Maybe I came back to show you I wasn't just a dumb broad, but someone who had some creativity too." Tears welled up. For a very private person, this admission was getting very close to home.

To get the conversation back onto a more neutral ground, Rose blundered on. "If I found out that there was no personal relationship possible, I was planning on trying to set up a business relationship."

It seemed as if this was the best chance of getting everything out in the open, so he encouraged her to continue by saying, "Business relationship?"

"Yes. I ran into a woman who liked my work. She said she had been doing a cut-out floral thing for years. Five years ago she advertized in *Architectural Digest.* She got tons of orders for her little thing and even today she picks up an occasional order because most people don't throw that magazine away. The whole scene has changed now because of the internet.

"When I was in LA, I went to the AD office to pick up the advertising rates for the Western Edition. Boy, are they steep. Anyway, I can afford it, but I need a permanent address, phone, fax, computer and shipping capability. You have all the things I need to get the business off the ground. I thought maybe we could work out a deal."

Zain continued to listen without comment.

After a pause, Rose forged on. "If we could get something

going together on a personal level, I'd be bringing something to the relationship and not be a financial liability."

Rose clamped her mouth shut, determined not to admit anything else until she had some feedback from Zain.

Zain reached across to take Rose's hands. "I'm so proud of you and your creativity in painting and in business I could bust. But......."

That statement was nice to hear, but that wasn't what Rose wanted to hear at that moment. She was holding her breath and when Zain said "but" she was ready to disintegrate into a defiant blob of self-pity.

"I wouldn't have cared if you were a non-creative financial liability, I'm glad you're back. Let's quit all this self-examination and start building the personal relationship you were talking about. It's you that interests me. In my eyes there is nothing wrong with you that I've been able to find. It was me, not you, that caused that standoff the last time."

Still Rose hesitated, debating about telling him her backup plan.

Zain noted her continued reluctance. He reached over to pat her hip. "I've even grown to like your tattoo. You have no idea the hours I spent recreating it in bas relief." He laughed at the thought.

Rose decided it was not time to address a situation that may never arise. "I'll bet it hurt me more than you." She slid off the seat onto her knees so they could embrace.

Even though there was a bed a few feet away, they ultimately decided that that wasn't the time for intimate expressions of their mutual commitment.

"What's the deal with *Architectural Digest?"* said Zain to get back into the current reality.

"I designed a tall, narrow ad showing one of my long driftwood paintings. Since each painting is different, I'll establish a website where available selections are displayed with thumbnail sketches, which can be brought to full-screen size. They can be purchased right on line."

"Are you planning to run the website or farm it out?"

"I'll try doing it myself, but if it gets in the way of production.....or lovemaking, I'll pass it on to someone else. This same thing should work for your sculptures too."

"It might, but for unknown big ticket items it would probably be a lot slower."

"What do you mean 'unknown'?"

"It's not like selling a car over the internet. With a car, the potential buyer can go find an example at a dealership or at least consult the local paper for comparables. My sculptures are unknowns and there are few places to find out about us. But, who knows if it will sell or not? It won't cost much to find out."

"There's one thing that concerns me," said Rose.

"What?"

"Colorado is a long ways from the source of driftwood. I suppose I could periodically make trips to the coast to collect materials."

"Let me show you something." said Zain, as he led Rose toward the welding studio. Along the way he stopped by the lumber pile where he sorted out an old, ragged 1x8. In the studio he tossed the board on the welding table, changed the welding tip to his largest, and fired up the torch. He started heavily charring the ends and the edges. He gave extra attention to the knots and the mars.

Wisps of carbon filled the studio. "This is better done outside," commented Zain as he turned off the torch. With a heavy nylon bristled brush he stroked along the gain revealing the raised hard grain of the wood. The soft grain had been burned away.

Rose watched intently. Where the edges of the driftwood were light in color, this process produced a rich black-brown color. Zain had left the interior portion of the wood unscathed.

"That looks great, but it's terribly smeary."

"That's no problem. Use liquid acrylic floor polish or flat acrylic varnish, depending on the effect you want."

Rose laid out her paints and started experimenting with the new board. Zain was trying to catch up on the orders from the shop. During the day it was a pretty good bet that at least one set of twins was somewhere around. Even Elen and Elsa, who were now third-graders wanted to be included in all the exciting happening in the big house.

Zain had drawn up plans for boxing in the next two stalls behind his sculpture studio as a painting studio for Rose. He also cut a door between the two facilities so they wouldn't have to go out into the cold to get back and forth.

Before any construction could begin, a mountain of plaster molds and their racks had to be moved. Rose said she'd leave all her things in Big Shack until everything was finished. That way nothing would have to be handled twice, and during the construction period she'd still be able to find things.

At breakfast on the tenth day after Rose's return, Zain proposed that they celebrate by going into town for dinner. Since he didn't take the local paper, he had no idea of what movies were playing so he said, "If we can find anything of interest, we can take in a movie too?"

"Gosh," said Rose. "I really don't have any dress-up clothes."

"I know a bunch of places where jeans are high fashion. Do you still have that little sombrero you used to wear on your ponytail?

"That one rotted out years ago."

"As soon as the kids get here, we have to pull three more waxes. I'll be in the studio."

Rose retired to Big Shack, but instead of painting, she went on a hunt until she found the little replacement sombrero she'd purchased ages earlier. She spent the rest of the morning cutting out the top and sewing on binding tape so it wouldn't fall apart.

When Zain saw the sombrero at lunch, he said, "Let's go to Chili's tonight." Rose nodded agreement, but Zain noted what he interpreted as a hesitancy. "If you don't want Mexican food we can go elsewhere."

"Mexican food is fine. I used to eat lots of it in southern California."

Zain was in a festive mood, but his companion wasn't sharing his enthusiasm. They skipped the movies and headed home for an intimate evening, which turned out to be the least enjoyable of their encounters. Rose was getting progressively more distant.

When Zain woke in the morning, he was alone in bed. Rose wasn't in the bathroom either. He quickly dressed and went downstairs. Rose was sitting at the kitchen table with a mug of coffee clasped in her hands.

"Hey, what's wrong? Have I said or done something to upset you?"

"No, it's not you."

"Then what?"

Rose got up, dumped her cold coffee in the sink and filled her mug and one for Zain.

Zain sat down across from Rose and tried to grasp her hands. She pulled away and turned sideways so she could look out the window.

Zain straightened his chair and quelled a flash of irritation. In a tone a little stronger that he had planned he said, "I'll ask again, what's wrong?"

Rose turned back and tried to pick up her mug, but she was shaking too hard. She stared at the coffee she'd sloshed onto the table. After a moment, she marshaled her reserves, stopped shaking and look Zain straight in the eye. "I lied to you. I'm not on the pill. I arrived during a fertile period and if things didn't work out, at least I'd have your baby."

Zain went rigid and became a shade paler. "You came here with the premeditated intent of stealing my son? I have a very strong proprietary interest in where my genes are spread. Is this some more of your liberal philosophy that what's yours is yours and what's mine is yours too?"

Rose fired back. "I have only so many eggs in my lifetime. And you can flush tens of thousands of your seed down the toilet every day until you're ancient. I just wanted one."

Zain lurched up from the table. His chair careened across the room putting the first dent in the decades old wood cook stove. He stormed out of the kitchen, slamming the mud room door so hard that the etched glass shattered.

Bleakly Rose watched as Zain disappeared. "Stupid bitch," she said aloud. "You've really done it now." Still maintaining her lock-jawed defiance. she stood up and headed upstairs. She reversed herself, picked up her heavy coffee mug and hurled it across the room putting a second dent in the cook stove.

While Rose was stuffing what few things she'd brought into the house into her knapsack, she heard the familiar cough of the antique Titan tractor. There was the ragged bark until the magneto was adjusted. Although buildings were in the way, she could tell the tractor was headed uphill at flank speed.

As Rose listened to her preferred future fading away in the distance, the tears began. Circumstances were always ganging up on her.

When the tractor fired up, Erik and Emil made a dive to get out of the barn, but Bo forcefully reminded them of their assigned duties. Never had the sacks been shifted from the truck to the granary so rapidly. Things were happening uphill and they were not a part of it.

Bo finally relented. The twins streaked up to the big house.

The cleated wheels of the tractor left an easily followed trail around the barn. Erik was in the lead. When he suddenly stopped, Emil crashed into him.

"What'cha doin'?" cried Emil.

Erik just pointed uphill before issuing the keening cry.

Emil refocused. The tractor hadn't gone through the gate, but plowed right through the fence on its journey uphill. Something was definitely wrong in their world.

The rest of the kids came racing up demanding to know what was happening.

"I don't know. Zain went right through the fence."

"Was Rose with him?" cried Inga

"Don't know. The tractor was out of sight before we go here. Go see if she's at the house. Ken, go tell dad the fence is down. The livestock can get out."

"Are you going to follow the tractor?" said Elsa.

Erik glanced toward his twin, who was shaking his head. "No, I don't think that would a good idea. He must really be mad. You girls find Rose. We'll check the studios."

Just as the kids started around the barn toward the house, there came a keening cry from Inga. As they rushed into sight of the house, they saw Inga standing by the closed door of Big Shack.

"When I came around the studio, Rose was sitting on the step crying. When she saw me, she picked up her knapsack and went inside and locked the door. She's pulling down all the window shades."

"Knock on the door," said Elen.

"I did and she won't answer."

"Try again," said Elen.

"You try. Maybe she'll open for you."

Elen climbed onto the step to rap on the door. Her little knuckles didn't make much sound so she shouted in a plaintive voice, "Rose, it's me. What's wrong. Was Zain bad to you?"

Erik hissed at her, “Don’t say that.”

“Why not? At school, Alice’s uncle is always beating Alice’s mother and they’re not married.”

Erik and Emil made a quick trip to the studios to make sure everything was in order. They rejoined their siblings at the big RV. They paired off and found somewhere to sit for the duration. The two youngest sets were holding each other. Inga and Inger were holding hands. The eldest were sitting on the back steps of the house but they were touching at the hips. They’d seen the broken back door window, which cast even a heavier gloom over their world.

When Zain stormed out the back door, he’d headed for the studio, which was his most favored place in the whole world. But, it was too close to his betrayer....Rose. When he spotted the tractor shed, he knew he’d found the perfect symbol of his contempt. He and Rose had spent many a weary hour on that beast in a worthy, common cause. Now he’d churn up the ground alone.

The roar of the great tractor was music to his ears. It deadened Rose’s voice in his head. Plowing down the fence was in keeping with his black mood. Nothing should get in his way.

Zain didn’t see any of the country side through which he passed. He was too intent on exploring the depths of her betrayal that he nearly plowed through the fence between his property and the BLM land. He came to a halt before the fence. Destroying the fence behind the barn had been a childish act of defiance. He didn’t want to make more work for himself, so Zain turned off the tractor and sat in the silence. High above him on the BLM land was a bare rock promontory he’d always wanted to climb. He’d thought it would be more fun to climb with someone else so the experience and beauty could be shared.

At the moment it seemed appropriate to do a solo climb. If he didn’t want to be used, he’d better get used to being alone.

He climbed over the fence and started up the mountain. As the going got harder more of his mental attention had to focus on the moment. By the time he reached the promontory, his legs were buzzing and he was gasping for breath.

He collapsed on a rock. The view was spectacular. It should have been shared. He would have loved to have done it with Rose, but she should be well on her way back to the beach. If she was, was she taking his son with her? If she was pregnant would she carry the baby to full term or flush him down the toilet like the rest of his seed?

And here he'd thought things were going so well. He had difficulty understanding such a sham. His eyes tracked back to his house. He concentrated because it looked as if Big Shack was still there. It was in the shadow of the house and difficult to see. Yes, it was still there....but why? Surely there was no benefit to be gained by hanging around. She'd already destroyed any chance that he'd ever trust her. She would just have to wait to see if her plan worked. If she hadn't gotten pregnant, she'd lose. If she was, she'd win. In either case he was a loser. So why was she still there?"

He'd had such high hopes that Rose would be the one. He thought she had shared those same hopes. She'd really had him fooled. He would have sworn that they were heading for a life together. He'd laid himself bare when he'd admitted why he'd gone looking for her. He thought she'd done the same when he'd asked why she'd come back. She'd only given reasons number two, three and four. So there was a lie of omission as well as the original sin of saying she was on the pill.

Zain focused again on the house. Big Shack was still there. Why? Was she having motor problems. That seemed unlikely. He wondered if the kids had gotten involved in their problem. They probably had tried, but this was none of their concern.

Why hadn't she left? Did she want another confrontation? He certainly didn't. Maybe she had to get in the final scream or whatever. It didn't seem reasonable that she she would try to put a patch over such a monstrous admission. If she'd really been working on a lasting relationship, she could have lied again. If she'd gotten pregnant, she could have simply shrugged it saying the pill was only 97% effective. If she wanted to stay on with him, that second lie would have passed unnoticed. All would have been well.

What did she say? "If things didn't work out at least I'd have your baby." What the hell does that mean? She must have been figuring it wasn't going to work out to admit she'd lied about the pill. If she wanted to have a kid, she could have found an agreeable stud anywhere. She said she practically had to drive them away with a stick. If she can't make a go of it with me, why would she want my son?

The sun was dropping further into the west. Big Shack was in deep shadow, but he could still make it out. If he didn't start back pretty soon, he'd be stumbling around in the dark.

After the roar of the tractor faded, Rose heard the keening cry from the direction of the barn. That meant the kids were around. She couldn't face them. When they disappeared behind the barn, Rose headed for the RV. As she started to open the door, she said, "What am I doing? I don't want to go." Her defiance started to slip and she plopped down on the step as tears started to flow again. Suddenly Inga was racing toward her. Oh, no, not now, thought Rose as she grabbed her knapsack and bolted into the RV.

After she pulled down the shades, she threw herself on the bed. She laid there without moving trying to get some psychic answer to the question of her possible pregnancy. Nothing came.

She came back to the present. "That pigheaded, straight-laced, egotistical, selfish, self-centered.....” She ran out of appropriate adjectives and finally ended with “bastard.”

Everything was going so well. Her world was coming together for once and then that arrogant bastard goes riding off into the sunset on their noble steed without waiting to get an explanation. Of course, she’d been wrong to have lied in the first place or committing the error of omission. She shouldn’t have taken such umbrage at his self-centered reaction, but those should have been reversible errors....if he’d stuck around long enough to listen. It was his petrified sense of propriety that foiled their first encounter and if she pulled the ignition key out of her jeans and drove away it would be their final encounter.

Rose hesitated after that thought. If she wasn’t pregnant, it would certainly end everything. But what would happen if she was pregnant? All this time she’d planned on simply disappearing and Zain would never know. But, now he knew there was a chance she could be carrying a baby away. That really complicated matters. Would he try to exercise parental rights? She’d never considered seeking any financial assistance. She’d do it all herself with her newly found talent. Of course, that could suddenly become a liability. He’d always be able to trace her through her art marketing. Everything was so complicated.

High above, Zain crawled over the fence and stood looking at the Titan. He didn’t want that roar in his head now. He wanted to think, so he started trudging downhill. The shadows were getting very long by the time he rounded the barn. Big Shack was there, as were four sets of twins.

On the way down the hill, Zain settled on what must be done. The twins all stood up, but they didn’t say anything. They were probably held in check by his stern expression and stiff-backed gate. As he approached the RV, Inga and Inger moved away from the steps. Zain struck a single heavy blow with the heel of his hand and said in something a little less than a shout, “Rose.”

Everyone waited. The seconds passed with no reaction. The kids began to fidget. After what seemed like an eternity, the lock snapped, but the door didn’t open. Zain pulled on the latch and the door came open. He climbed the steps, entering the dim interior closing the door after him. The kids could hear the murmur of voices but they couldn’t overhear what was being said. Inga and Inger settled back down on the steps. The rest sat down again.

Carina served dinner for Bo and herself. She hadn’t called the kids. They had their own problem. She’d received reports through the afternoon as various of her offspring made bathroom calls.

Rose was seated at the table. Zain slid onto the bench across from her. Even in the gloom he could see she’d been crying. She didn’t say anything. Zain said softly, “Why are you still here?”

“I couldn’t leave.”

“Why?”

“I had to explain.”

“I’m glad to hear that. I can’t understand any of this. I thought everything was going so well.”

“Me too.”

“Then how come you dropped that bomb right in the middle of it? That’s one of the things I don’t understand. If you really wanted this to work out, then you could have been surprised at a pregnancy. I would have been ecstatic. But, no, you had to lay out your plot. Didn’t you think I would react?”

“Yes. I figured you’d react, but I also figured you’d hang around long enough to hear the rest.”

“What rest?”

“I told you earlier that one of the reasons I came back was to find out if there was something wrong with me. In all the time we spent together I couldn’t raise a single spark out of you. It's been bothering me ever since. In all those months I decided I wanted you....you, but if I couldn't have you, I wanted your baby. That was the thinking behind plan B, the baby."

"There's a bunch of guys out there that would be more than happy to give you a son, so why pick me?"

The fire came back into Rose's eyes. "I'm just as fussy as you about spreading my genes. Oh, there are a whole bunch of magnificent male specimens at Muscle Beach. Alexer, the sculptor at Garibaldi probably would have accommodated me if I'd asked. But, I wanted your genes to mix with my genes. You have an adequate body, your looks pass the test, but the important part is what's between your ears....your intellect, your creativity, your sensitivity, your personality, you. That's why I wanted to mix your genes with mine."

"Wouldn't it be better to have me on the scene? It's hard to raise a son without a male model."

"What's this thing with sons? Would you care if I had a daughter?"

Zain gave her a rather funny look. "Zooks don't have daughters....normally. I have a female second cousin, but I think that's the only one. We have boys....like the Vasas have twins. I'd never thought of having a daughter. In my family, a girl would be spoiled rotten. But, that's not the point. I want to raise my own progeny."

"You should."

"Then why screw it all up?" Zain was getting agitated again. "How could you......."

"Oh, shut up you blockhead and listen," shouted Rose in a volume that carried out to the kids. They cringed.

Rose lowered her voice. "Yes, I could have done as you say, ignored my lie and forget about my error of omission, but I couldn't have lived with that. I'd never be content with that on my conscience. I would have gotten you under false pretenses. I couldn't have lived with that guilty knowledge. Eventually, it would have ripped us apart. It's better to get it out now than after there's all sorts of legal matters to worry about."

Zain sat for sometime without saying anything. Then he reached across the table to grip Rose's hands. She didn't pull away. "How can I fault that kind of integrity? You know, I could never claim victory either under that scenario. Where do we stand? Does each of us have to apologize for his transgressions or can we say that they were just plays of the first half? It is behind us and forgotten. The score is zero to zero and now we can look to the second half."

Rose smiled at his analogy. "I'm game if you are. How do we start this half?"

"Why don't we go back there." Zain jerked his head toward the bedroom in the rear. We can work on that son again. Tomorrow I'll call Judge Winters to see if he can come up this weekend to make everything official, so that when our son comes along people won't start counting on their fingers."

Inga stood up. She put her hand on the side of Big Shack. "Oh, they're breeding."

"They must like each other again," said Elen.

It was too dark to mime, so Kas announced, "I'm hungry.

"Me, too," declared Emil.

Moments later all eight twins were trooping home.

Epilogue

The Sunday afternoon wedding was a private, arty affair. Zain had suggested the studio as an appropriate location, but he deferred to Rose, who wanted the music room so the girls could play the piano.

Of course, the judge presided. Pam hired a baby sitter so as not inflict her kids on the celebrants. Besides, she wanted a break.

Carina solved the dress question. To keep her brood from having to appear in their age-specific mod school clothes, she suggested the entire entourage dress in gray gym attire. The boys wore bottoms and the girls tops....adults wore both tops and bottoms. The only exceptions to the dress code were the Winters because of political considerations.

Carina helped Rose remodel her attire by making short-short, low-rise shorts and a short top to show as much of her tattoo as propriety allowed.

Bo looked rather strange in his farmer's tan. Devon brought his current flame, who provided a workshop for the girls on how to show her date everything she had while appearing to be a model of modesty. Hunter managed to swagger even in gym togs. He was also able to surreptitiously direct his photographer to catch every action from the appropriate angle.

Pam had a great day. She found a couple of new targets to tease....Kas and Ken. She kept their ears aglow all afternoon.

Rose insisted that the "Victory" sculpture with the roses

be brought down to stand with her. Erik and Emil were best men and Inga and Inger did double duty as maids-of-honor and pianists who played their four-hand version of the wedding march. Rose held a contented smile during the festivities. However, Zain wore a broad smirk because Rose had advised him of a positive reaction to her pregnancy test.

Carina had prepared an enormous summer picnic style meal in Zain's kitchen. It was served on the big veranda front porch because everyone, except the kids, were too tender footed to stomp about the yard. Zain didn't have a lawn as such.

The newlyweds spent their first night at home but left early in the morning in Big Shack. It had been stripped of all non-essential weight so a load of Pacific driftwood could be hauled home.

978982004425

www.ingramcontent.com/pod-product-compliance
Lightning Source LLC
LaVergne TN
LVHW091048080826
845145LV00002B/661

* 9 7 8 0 9 8 2 0 0 4 4 2 5 *